I0778869

When Araminta Greaves Traded Her Dignity For Bliss

Wainwright Sisters Book One

Andrea Jenelle

Copyright © 2023 by Andrea Jenelle

All rights reserved.

No part of this publication may be reproduced, distributed, or transmitted in any form or by any means, including photocopying, recording, or other electronic or mechanical methods, without the prior written permission of the publisher, except as permitted by U.S. copyright law. For permission requests, contact [include publisher/author contact info].

The story, all names, characters, and incidents portrayed in this production are fictitious. No identification with actual persons (living or deceased), places, buildings, and products is intended or should be inferred.

Book Cover by Period Images, Inc.

Print ISBN-13: 978-1-962123-02-0
Digital ISBN-13: 978-1-962123-03-7

First edition 2023

To every reader who believes in the magic of the holidays, Hallmark movie endings, fuzzy socks, someone who brings you tea and takes you for sleighrides, and letting go so you can become the best version of yourself. And of course to everyone else who wanted a spicier version of Maria and Capt. Von Trapp's love story.

TABLE OF CONTENTS

A Whirling Dervish Out of Whirl

December 1861 - Cumbria, England

She always chose dignity over bliss. It was much safer because her heart wouldn't break.

She told herself she preferred logic over superstition and flights of fancy. Rational, scientific observation over imaginary omens. Things she could verify with her five senses. Not mere supposition and guessing and wildly improbable speculation.

If a black cat crossed her path, she didn't cling to the edge of the woodland like a ninny and risk falling into a patch of wild blackberry brambles in an effort to avoid it. She didn't spiral into a panic and wonder what its appearance *meant*. Instead, she scooped it up and scratched its ears until it was quiescent and purring in her arms.

She firmly believed salt was a precious commodity. She wasn't about to throw it over her shoulder and waste it to ward off imaginary specters. She didn't have fond memories of trying to make bare cupboards stretch and producing palatable food for her finicky younger sisters after their mother died.

But this week had been marked by miniature disasters she couldn't afford to ignore. One after the other in rapidly escalating succession. They loomed over her like the screeching bats that rippled across the grounds when their attic roost was disturbed - harbingers of horrors to come.

First, she'd lost her watch fob. It had a small pewter heart charm engraved with the inscription, *Always*. She'd been a gangly, awkward bookworm on the cusp of womanhood when her mother had pressed it into the palm of her hand and whispered, "Let this remind you that no one is impervious their entire lives. Your father wooed me way from everything I knew, and his devotion has been unfailing. When my death makes him hard and brittle, rub your thumb over this word and give him as much grace as you can."

It was the only memento she had of the softness that surrounded her childhood. A reminder of the moment her path diverged from innocent youth to the bleak maturity suddenly thrust upon her shoulders. Her mother's death from puerperal fever in the childbed had turned her father into a harsh, unforgiving man who barely spared she and her sisters three words in a day. He'd viewed his daughters as unwanted reminders of his dead wife and treated them like nothing more than commodities to be bartered at the village market.

She very seldom removed the pendant with the charm dangling from it. It was her lodestone and a reminder she could always hope for a future filled with more. With something brighter.

She'd looked everywhere for it. The chicken coop. The rubbish bin. The vast space beneath her bed. There'd been nothing there but tiny piles of dust. It was like it had been sucked into the ether - like a stocking mysteriously gone missing from the wash, never to be seen again. She was heartbroken at the loss. It was the last bit of dreaming left in her life gone forever.

The very next morning, one of the scullery maids tripped over a fat mouser slumbering in the kitchen doorway and shattered six dozen eggs across the flagstone. Her stepson was insufferable because he had to go a single morning without coddled eggs. Their absence turned him into even more of a tyrant – berating the servants for the slightest infraction and railing about the imagined indignities he suffered at the hands of his neighbors. Everyone in the household had given him a wide berth for the entire day.

Two days after the egg incident, one of the always underfoot hounds attacked the hem of one of her last remaining dresses. His antics completely rent the seams in the arms and bodice. It would be impossible to replace the threadbare fabric until after the holidays. Which left her with a grand total of three dresses including the one she was obliged to wear to church on Sundays or when she was supervising social events like tonight's ball.

A day after the dress fiasco, one of the new footmen found a nest of hibernating snakes in the wine cellar when he was sent to retrieve a bottle of port. Terrified, he stumbled into one of the racks and sent it crashing to the floor. Not only had it taken hours to clean up, but it was also the reason no madeira was being served tonight.

The afternoon immediately following the madeira disaster, one of the arborists miscalculated the angle of the giant oak he was cutting down for firewood. When it fell, it went straight through the roof of the hunting lodge at the edge of the woods. The cold and rain meant the roof couldn't be repaired for at least two weeks. And a roof in disrepair meant she had no bolt hole. The lodge was where she escaped when she had a few hours to ignore everything but the book she was reading. It was the one place she could let the worry that was her constant companion melt away like lemon drops.

Yesterday morning, the footmen lost their grasp on the heavy gilt framed mirror they'd removed from the ballroom mantel for cleaning. The shards had flown across the polished floor and two of the staff had wasted an entire day ensuring all of them were hunted down and disposed of because they were hazardous to dancing slippers. There were dark murmurs of seven years of cursed bad luck and speculation about whose shoulders it would fall upon. (Most of the household believed it would be her since she was the one who'd ordered the mirror removed.)

And lastly, this morning had brought the most ominous portent of all. An entire murder of ravens had been perched in the bare, gloomy branches outside her window. They'd glared at her while she leaned against the casement and grimly sipped her tea. If you asked anyone else they would say those perching ravens meant her future was doom and gloom. She'd morbidly reflected they may as well be an outward manifestation of the darkness in her soul she was constantly fighting.

Those ravens with their hoarse admonitions and shiny black feathers were beautiful because they could fly away. They weren't trapped in an exhausting round of days in a space that would never truly welcome her. That promise of freedom was why she'd refused to believe all of the doomsayers that muttered about tonight's event. They knew she had no tolerance for old wives' tales and clammed up when she walked into a room, but she knew they'd placed bets on just how disastrous it would be.

No, she wasn't superstitious. But even she was hard pressed to ignore the ravens.

Was their arrival some harbinger of the fate she shouldn't be ignoring? What if the inaugural holiday party she'd planned down to every last scrupulous detail was a fiasco? Or worse yet, a disaster? What if it made her stepson's wife a laughingstock instead of cementing her reputation as the reigning queen of county society? Arie shuddered to think how that outcome would impact her. If the superstitions of everyone else involved in the preparations proved correct, all the blame for the failure, no matter what form it took, would fall on her shoulders.

Many A Thing They Ought to Understand

Thaddeus St. Simon found it very difficult to tell his children no. A virtually impossible feat, in fact. They were motherless after all. If he'd stayed home instead of going to war, tragedy might have been averted. His wife might still be alive and they would still have a mother. But instead of staying home he marched away and was promptly dispatched to the Crimea. He spoiled them to make amends for his abandonment. And now he was paying the price for his indulgence.

He felt guilty for surviving the war while half his family died of diphtheria. Because he wasn't there to wipe their brows, or kiss their foreheads or bury them. He let them run roughshod over him in his pursuit for benediction. He knew he should be assessing the ranks of single women to find a woman willing to take both himself and his mischievous children on, but he couldn't muster the desire. There was only one woman he'd even consider worth the effort, and she barely knew he existed and was wrapped in widow's weeds.

This evening the twins, Rissa and Callie, and his youngest, Claire, had clung to his trousers like barnacles. Eleven-year-old Clementine watched from the corner and failed to hide her giggles behind her hand.

He'd tried, in vain, to explain the party he was attending was for adults, not children. That explanation hadn't silenced them. It had prompted a barrage of questions instead about when he was going to secure a mother for them. Was he bringing her home tonight? The twins mutinously insisted they expected him to secure one as their holiday gift. When he'd asked why the sudden haste, they'd indignant-ly admitted their grandmother made them wear shoes and wouldn't let them go fishing. When he'd asked what their criteria for a mother was, the only requirements the twins had given him were tree-climbing skills, a lovely laugh, a scent like the flower garden in spring. Claire's only demand had been the ability to give hugs that were wonderful but not tight enough to crush your bones.

By the time he'd finally quelled the insurrection and calmed them down with a promise to return home with a sampling of all the desserts and a vow to dance with at least three prospective candidates for motherhood, the festivities were well under way. Thad handed his card to the footman but tried to make his entry as unnoticeable and seam-less as possible. He quickly spotted his quarry in the corner. Contrary to his daughters' belief, his objective in attending the rout was not to find a new wife. His goal was to finally convince his recalcitrant neighbor to relinquish the prime acreage that served as a boundary between their holdings.

Mr. Johnston had refused to consider the sale of the forty hectares bordering the field Thad kept his ewes in. He had it on good authority the man lived above his means and liked to gamble. His determination to refuse a perfectly viable offer with the potential to alleviate some of his financial woes was inexplicable. Thad suspected it was either pride or some other pressure the man didn't care to share. The pride of some people was so misplaced it was baffling, but at least it was something he could assuage and navigate around. If there were shadier reasons influencing the man's reluctance Thad intended to ferret them out.

He had no illusions about the parish's perception of him. He may have served his country and returned as a war hero, but he was still too big, scarred, intense and curt for polite company. He demanded too much and didn't believe in standing on ceremony. He was too eager to embrace new-fangled farming methods and too unwilling to give deference to those who believed they were his social betters. He'd never seen the point in fawning obsequiousness, and though he hadn't attended Oxford or Cambridge, his father was a respected physician and made certain he was well-schooled in philosophy and the sciences. He'd made use of his learning. He'd invested the small bequest made to him by his grandmother in railroads and earned enough to purchase his farm outright. He was steadily adding to his holdings and his stock. The forty hectares he was trying to wheedle from Johnston would make him one of the most substantial landowners in the county.

When he'd joined the troops headed to Sevastopol, his neighbors had morosely shaken their heads and bemoaned his abandonment of his family. He'd joined to add to the nest egg he'd made from his investments, and his wife had supported his decision. Their brood already numbered seven and she'd been increasing again. He'd been adamant about expanding their farm operations and he'd needed more connections and capital to do it. Sequestered in their corner of Cumbria, he was hemmed in by families who'd held sway over local politics and land transactions for centuries. The realization of his dreams had meant he needed support and backing from elsewhere. He'd figured a berth in Her Majesty's Army would at least allow him the opportunity to find potential investors. He'd thought his family would be safe in his absence.

Rachel had the ready assistance of both sets of grandparents to dote on their seven children. She'd given him every assurance she was an old hat at bearing his brats and her swollen belly would pose no problems. She reiterated that she'd married him for his sense of honor and justice and his new offspring would welcome their father home.

He still wondered if he would've been spared the cold churchyard or perished alongside his wife and three eldest children. The diphtheria that had taken them from him had left a wide wake of sorrow through the entire village. His daughters survived because they'd been spending a month with their cousins in Shropshire and had been isolated from the onset of the disease in their siblings.

He'd mused if the Scottish surgeon he'd occasionally shared cigars with during the war had the right of it. The man had insisted the cause of diphtheria and other diseases like it was rooted in the spread of airborne foul humors he called bacteria. The survival of his daughters bore out this theory because they'd been visiting cousins in the neighboring county when the outbreak happened. He was certain they were alive because they'd been spared exposure to the sickness..

Determined to get an answer about the land he'd been badgering his neighbor about, he strode toward him. Johnston flinched at his approach and Thaddeus was certain he would've scurried away, if he hadn't lunged forward and caught the edge of the man's sleeve. "I want to know why you've been avoiding me, Johnston. And why you're refusing a perfectly reasonable offer."

The man gaped up at him. Apparently Thaddeus's blunt question wasn't de rigeur in a social setting. Given Thad's reputation, his forthright manner shouldn't have been a surprise. "Ah, St. Simon," Johnston finally sputtered in response.

Thaddeus raised a brow at his discomfiture. The brow must've spoken volumes because the tips of the man's ears turned scarlet, and he nervously twisted his hands in front of him. "I can't sell to you, St. Simon."

"Why not? I know you can use the funds." The man's refusal made no sense. He had it on good authority Johnston was surreptitiously pawning everything on his estate not bolted down in order to pay off his gambling debts.

Johnston pulled himself up to his full height, and still barely reached the middle of Thad's chest. "My debts are none of your concern."

Thad snorted. They might not be his concern, but the entire village knew the man and his family were headed for penury and would soon be out on their arses. "No, I warrant they aren't. But you could still use it to purchase new frocks for your passel of daughters or buy livestock for your home farm." Or pay off your debts and use the respite to learn how to live more modestly and avoid games of chance, he silently added.

"I can't sell it to you." The popinjay belligerently reiterated, tugging on the lace at his sleeves.

Thad's gaze narrowed with suspicion. "Can't or won't?"

Johnston sighed. "Both. I won't sell it to you because I have no wish to anger another party. I can't sell it to you because I would lose the beneficence of that other party."

Thad had a decent inkling of the identity of the other party. He and the current lord of the manor had been at odds since puberty and this was just their latest run-in, oblique though it was. Squire Hugh Greaves was both competitive and petty. If Johnston's acreage was added to the St. Simon holdings, Thad would have almost as much land as the parish's largest landowner. And he knew Hugh well enough to know he would never allow that to happen. He'd always believed his social status as the son of the largest landowner guaranteed him certain privileges. Privileges Thad was now encroaching on. "So the squire's opposed, is he?"

Johnston gaped again. Like trout with a hook lodged in its jowl. "Make sure he knows you didn't hear it from me."

He just shook his head at the man's consternation. He'd spent his entire adult life running interference for everyone who found themselves in Hugh's sights. He'd even wondered at the fate of Hugh's stepmother. He remembered accompanying his father to her mother's sickbed and imagining her bound to the lecherous old squire had made his skin crawl and the gorge rise in his throat. He'd been a guest at her wedding nearly twelve years ago and pulled her into a jig. The banns had been read and he'd been on the verge of exchanging his vows with Rachel – but he could still feel the ghost of her in his arms and the puff of her breath against his neck as he twirled her around. He remembered how lovely she'd been and how much he'd wanted to spin her off into the night to get her away from her husband's wandering hands. He'd pitied the misery of her situation and the loss of the carefree girl he'd once known.

"So you're fixed on your course?" Thad prodded.

The man gulped and vigorously shook his head. "You must understand I have no choice. I hope there will be no hard feelings between us."

Thad snorted. "You're asking for my charitable understanding of the delicacy of your situation?"

"I'd be much obliged," he held out his hand for gentlemanly assurance.

"I don't feel like sealing our understanding with a handshake, old chap," Thad smacked his shoulder so hard the man lurched sideways. He quickly righted himself and glowered.

"You're not a gentleman, St. Simon."

Thad shrugged. "I never claimed to be. But what I will always be is fair and honest. No matter who I'm dealing with. But those are character defects in your eyes and those of the company you keep. Which means I won't be shaking your hand. Now or ever. I wish you luck resolving your situation." He gave a jaunty salute and strode in the opposite direction.

With the reason for his attendance thwarted, he had no desire to promenade reluctant partners around the ballroom. He'd just tell his daughters there were no likely prospects. He'd grab the desserts he'd promised the girls he'd being home and be on his way. He now saw his failure had been inevitable. Hugh had the man's balls in an iron vise and no amount of inducement or cajoling would be sufficient to wrest him away.

He was halfway across the room when he noticed her. The stepmother who shouldn't be a stepmother. Who shouldn't be dressed in black or stuck in a corner. He steadfastly endeavored not to notice her at these events and always failed. She certainly didn't notice him. He doubted she was aware of his existence.

He remembered her before she became a wife. How forlorn she looked at her wedding. He remembered the soft weight of her in his arms, pressed flush for an infinitesimal moment when he twirled her beneath the lights.

Before she became a widow. Before and after she was motherless.

He remembered watching the dusty bottoms of her bare feet pelt across the green and kick into the air as she propelled her swing toward the sky with pointed toes. He remembered glimpsing the furious flap of her dark braid down her back as she dipped in and out of alleys, around the corners of buildings, weaving through the crowd on market day. He remembered the way his seventeen-year-old heart stuttered in his chest when she was bathed in the hazy, shimmering light of a summer afternoon.

He remembered how her hand had fallen from the loose clasp of her mother's and flown to her mouth to hold in a sob.

He remembered how somber she'd been at her wedding to the squire three times her age. All her infectious joy cast aside in the name of duty.

He remembered how she looked in the village church every Sunday. Her spine erect, her hands clasped tightly in her lap. No hint of the mischief or joy that had once been her default expression.

She was quietly ensconced in her usual corner and he decided to take advantage of the opportunity. He maneuvered his way around the periphery of the whirling couples, intent on pulling her with him into the melee of dancers.

Her eyes were bottomless wells of dark peat, with striations of gunmetal gray around her irises. They widened as he bore down on her. He reluctantly acknowledged it was because he alarmed her, not because she recognized him. He came to a halt, the gleaming tips of his boots touching her own sturdy footwear.

"Tell me, Mrs. Greaves, do you climb trees?"

She tilted her head and furrowed her brow. Like he'd asked if she preferred to drink ratafia straight from the punch bowl or ride ostriches across the desert. Her eyes sparkled up at him. "Well, sir, I've been known to scale quite the towering specimen in my day."

He had the sudden urge to close his eyes as an image of her scaling him flitted through his mind.

She narrowed her gaze. "I don't believe we are well enough acquainted to answer such impertinent questions."

He doffed his hat. "Thaddeus St. Simon at your service. It's likely too much to hope that you're a proficient angler as well."

"As it so happens, sir, I am quite the angler. And with nothing more than a cane pole, and a bit of string I've caught quite the loveliest dinner."

Two of the twins' requirements fulfilled. She was still a country lass at heart and would be understanding of their restless spirit. "One last question, Mrs. Greaves."

"I wait with bated breath." She sarcastically quipped.

He bent nearer, and the scent of violets filled his nostrils. He wanted to brush away the tendrils of hair that curled just past her ears, damp with perspiration. The last requirement was of a more delicate nature. "What of your hugs? Are they bone-crushing or merely fortifying and restorative?"

Her gaze narrowed and he wanted to squirm like a schoolboy summoned to the front of the classroom. Like a worm gutted by one of her fishing hooks. "Save your outrageous flirtation for a woman not inured to flattery and temptation."

"I do not believe..."

She waved a hand to cut him off and nodded firmly. He stepped forward to reassure her that it wasn't exactly flirtation and she stepped back with a warning glare. Their awkward shuffle was interrupted by a horrific yowl.

"Oh dear!" She exclaimed and thrust her half-full cup into his hands as she looked over his shoulder and scurried away. He thought he heard her mutter *of course the ravens were right.*

He turned toward the table laden with a crystal punch bowl and platters full of delicacies. A cream comfit was within his grasp when all hell broke loose.

Something thudded into the middle of his back, and he fell forward, collapsing onto the table. The stack of plates went flying into the air, one of his fists plowed through the middle of a fruitcake, and the punch bowl leapt off the lopsided surface and shattered on the floor. His coat was covered in confection and ratafia. The desserts were ruined and there was no salvaging them. So much for stuffing his pockets full of contraband for his daughters. He'd have to distract them with an animated accounting of the utter chaos that ended the party. They'd be amused that everything was because of the strife between the cats and dogs. Sound effects would be necessary if he hoped to rivet them enough they didn't pout at the lack of desserts.

When he stripped off the jacket and turned around, he was almost knocked over again. The swarm of dancers was stampeding the arched entry, desperate to escape the descent of the gargantuan tree that had been standing sentry in the corner. Its descent was the cause of the panicked exit, even though most of the crowd was well out of range. The disaster was even more reason for an early departure and he decided he'd escape to the stables and saddle Roland himself.

How Do You Solve a Problem

When Arie saw the orange paw brazenly slide from under the towering tree and latch onto the snout of one of the ever-present, always underfoot, hunting hounds, she wasn't immediately alarmed. And then the squealing and growling became loud enough to drown out all conversation when the hound reared back with the cat attached. The banshee shriek of the enraged mouser scrambling to disengage echoed from the damask covered walls and every gilt rose adorning the ruby red plaster ceiling. And then the bowels of hell erupted into the ballroom, and she vowed to rename the troublemaker Beelzebub. She'd been enjoying her banter with the tall, scarred gentleman and resented the interruption. She'd been certain he was on the verge of asking her to dance – if her rebuff hadn't frightened him off.

The tree swayed dangerously, and some of the dried fruits and tiny presents lodged in its branches toppled to the parquet floor. The shriek increased in crescendo as the tabby cat streaked from under its hiding place and the baying hounds lumbered after it.

She was grateful she'd had the foresight to deny her stepdaughter-in-law's petulant request to add candles to the tree branches. She hadn't refused because of the danger. She'd refused because she wasn't going to create additional housekeeping duties for herself and the staff. Especially when she knew they would result in the painstaking removal of puddled wax drippings from the parquet floors after the guests took their leave. So she refused.

The reaction to her refusal had been a stony, pouting wall of silence punctuated by outlandishly irrational demands. The tightrope she'd been walking between meeting those demands and preserving her sanity and that of the rest of the household staff had been wearing her down, and she'd been questioning the wisdom of her decision. Until now. Now she knew her decision had been completely justified. She wanted to pat herself on the shoulder for her prescience, because her determination to resist meant several guests were safely scurrying away from the leaning tree instead of going up in flames.

She watched in abject horror as the tree began to lean even more precariously, unbalanced as the prime mouser from the stables reeled towards it and began scrabbling to the top. One of the hounds, not to be denied of its quarry, attempted to scrabble up right behind it. Underneath the screeching and scuffling she heard an unmistakable giggle. She immediately knew who the culprits behind the mischief were. She'd bet all the pin money she didn't have that Ruby, the eldest of her incorrigible step-granddaughters, was the chief instigator.

Something ominously groaned. It may have come from the tree as it sprang free of the ropes tethering it to the wall. It may have been her own gasp of mortified fascination. It may have been the hysterical squeals of the guests as they shoved each other out of the way in their haste to escape being squashed. Even the village gossip, who preferred to have her companion fan her in a corner so she could complain of her gout to anyone within listening distance, scurried out of the way. They looked like ants in an absurd circus charade chasing after the last crumbs from a picnic blanket vigorously shaken out. Even the ones green about the gills from their consumption of the Angels on Horseback oyster hors d'oeuvres.

One of the hounds veered into the footman's knees standing directly in front of her. He fought to maintain his balance, but it was a desperate gamble. His sharp elbow covered in cerulean blue fustian arrowed towards her before she had a chance to duck. She'd waylaid him because some of the guests who'd eaten the oysters had taken ill. They were likely spoiled and needed to be removed and switched out immediately.

She couldn't avoid the elbow or the footman. They both ended up on the floor. His elbow struck her nose and it hurt like she'd been flattened by the famous boxer Gentleman Jim. Her injured appendage was gushing blood like a geyser, and both her dress and his livery were liberally sprayed with scarlet.

She tried to catch her breath on the edge of the ballroom, prostrate and covered in dripping blood and dripping oysters. Her black bombazine, the very last in her possession without a trampled hem and frayed cuffs, would now be relegated to the back of her pathetically scant wardrobe until she could figure out a way to repair the damage. The only saving grace to the collision was that the lack of a proper gown excused her from the vicar's parsimonious, hellfire and brimstone Sunday sermons. She always had the inkling suspicion that he could see the rebellion stirring in her soul and whenever he preached about duty, he was directing his admonitions at her.

She had reluctantly agreed to serve as a behind-the-scenes conductor for this event. Violet, her stepson's wife, wanted to impress her neighbors with her status by flaunting a magnificent adoption of the holiday customs practiced at Windsor. The luxuriously adorned tree, the groaning table full of food, the four days of rollicking festivities she had planned, all were a plea for the world to turn its envious eyes on her magnificence. If the woman could've found a Tiny Tim to serve as her mascot, she would have snatched him up on the spot. Propriety and taking advantage of the village poor be damned.

The only snag in Violet's grand scheme was her woeful ineptitude at pulling off such an endeavor. She knew nothing about running a household or planning an event of this magnitude, and her arrogance had alienated everyone below the stairs. She resented the fact that she had to ask Arie, her deceased father-in-law's third wife, to step in and ensure the whole thing went off without a hitch.

When Arie had reluctantly taken the helm, she'd known if things went awry and the ball was not a roaring success, somehow the blame would be laid at her feet. She had no choice but to agree she was ideally suited to organize the entire event and do everything in her power to ensure things went according to plan.

Arie was always the one who orchestrated everything behind the scenes. She was expected to be inobtrusive, competent and unflappable. She was expected to smooth over any awkwardness or unpleasantness for the rest of the household and then fade obediently into the background once again. Which she strove to do- even when her black garb stood out in harsh relief against the garish wall coverings. Like an ugly horsehair sofa everyone forgot about because it was an eyesore until its cushions needed plumped or its sturdy clawfoot legs collided with unsuspecting toes.

She'd had her own reasons for agreeing to manage the chaos unraveling before her eyes. At least it gave her the chance to discreetly tipple excellent sherry in an alcove and compose imaginary scandalous back stories for all the staid denizens of parish society. That respite had escaped her tonight. She'd managed one sip before her interruption from the farmer the size of a small oak tree.

This entire doomed event reminded her why she loathed balls. They never went according to plan.

She wrenched herself to her feet, dripping oysters, and every last shred of her dignity, onto the Aubusson carpet beneath her feet. Cleaning the silk fibers of the rug would be a nightmare.

He looked aghast at causing the collision and was just as green around the gills as the guests who'd eaten the oysters. He obviously feared repercussions for the collision. "Ma'am, my humblest apologies," he stuttered as he tried to ineffectually use his neckcloth to clean her gown.

"I thought we were on a first name basis, Ivan," she chastised him. "You may call me Arie like everyone else." She had a rapport with everyone that kept things running smoothly because they knew she was like them. She hadn't been born to the manor, so to speak. She'd been plucked from the ignominy of the muddy roads and tiny cottages their own families lived in.

She was an object of unabashed wonder and speculation. Somehow she'd escaped the muddy roads. There was an embarrassing familiarity because the servants had once seen her pelting down those muddy roads barefoot. They never quite succeeded in disguising their pity because they all recognized and sympathized with the reality that she was at the manor on forbearance and could be cast back into those muddy roads at any moment.

Ivan blushed. "What shall you do, ma'am?" he asked, finally abandoning his futile efforts with the neckcloth.

The guests were running around like a pack of distracted school children let loose in a menagerie, gawping at the industrial wonders of the Great Exhibition or the treasures extracted from an Egyptian pyramid. "We have to get the tree upright again. You and the other four footmen need to wrestle it back in the corner. I'll recruit Molly and the other two scullery maids to help me discreetly remove the oysters from circulation so they can go to the midden heap. Griggs," she beckoned to the distraught butler, "You need to shepherd the guests into the large parlor. Calm their nerves and distract them with the cold foodstuffs and mulled wine while the rest of us clean up the ballroom."

The butler, Griggs, gave her an appalled look. "But ma'am. What of your gown?"

"There's no help for it. 'Tis likely ruined and will smell of oysters forever. Once we have things under control, I'll have to retire and change into my black wool for the night as the only other acceptable gown I own is out for laundering." She shrugged her shoulders. "Griggs, you are perfectly capable of handling things in the drawing room, so please cease wringing your hands. It is your duty to ensure everyone acts with consummate aplomb and you must set the tone for the rest of us."

The bewildered man shakily nodded his head. Then he straightened his shoulders, the steel of his spine evident once again, and assumed his usual unflappable expression.

She turned to Molly and the other downstairs maids who had just come to a huffing, puffing, breathless stop in front of her. "You three are with me. Make sure you gather all the oyster platters as quickly and discreetly as possible and take them back down to the kitchen. By my count, the punch bowl has been emptied at least seven times, so I think the guests will be oblivious to the removal."

"Oh, and Griggs, you'll need to ensure the guests who've complained after eating the oysters are guided to their rooms. Please send for Dr. Quarles if you deem it necessary."

"I agree that we need to remove them before they render themselves immobile from more wine," he paused, tapping one knuckle swollen with rheumatism against his chin, "I believe I shall go ahead and send for Dr. Quarles. I'll advise him that he'll be handsomely compensated if he can stay for the duration of the party."

"I believe that would be wise," she agreed. The young doctor was newly arrived in the parish and had already made his determination to enter the ranks of well-heeled society evident to all and sundry. He wouldn't turn down a way to line his pockets and an opportunity to rub elbows with those he sought to infiltrate.

"Ma'am," he clasped his hands in front of him. "Mayhap Lady Heron's abigail can clean your dress. Shall I summon her to your rooms when you retire?"

She wanted to snort at the absurdity of his suggestion. It was well-meaning but highly unlikely. Violet Heron Greaves guarded the services of her abigail like the troll manning the bridge from Grimm's Three Billy Goats Gruff. She was more likely to bare her teeth and gobble up anyone who dared impugn her by asking for Alice's assistance.

Despite the fact this particularly lavish affair was being held in her home and she was the mistress of ceremonies, she knew her only recourse would be to scrub it out in the laundry sink herself and hope for the best. She knew her efforts would be fruitless. The gown and her dignity belonged in the midden heap with the bad oysters.

"Please find your way to the music room. Light refreshments will be provided," the butler shouted over the hubbub.

Confident Griggs had shepherding the guests well in hand, she gestured for the maids to follow her. The footmen were heaving the tree upright once again, but it was now devoid of most of the adornments that had completely obscured the branches.

***

When Arie finally crept up the stairs she encountered the wide-eyed fascination of her step-grandchildren. She was exhausted and still stank of sweat and oysters. She hadn't managed to slip away to put herself to rights and all she wanted was the glass of sherry circumstances had denied her and ten minutes to elevate her sore feet. Cleaning up the mess wrought by the cavorting creatures had taken up most of the evening.

Although she resented the necessity of the duty and the vulnerability of her position as their governess, she welcomed the responsibility because it gave her the opportunity to teach the girls useful things that would stand them in good stead if they were bartered off like she'd been. Things she knew their mother would heartily disapprove of if she bothered to pay attention. Like picking the perfect cane pole, climbing trees and chasing butterflies. Their inquisitiveness and enthusiasm were the only brightness in a life otherwise marked by dreary rooms, tepid tea, and isolation.

The girls were ensconced along the balcony, avidly watching the ruckus they'd caused, their legs swinging through the slats of the railing. A late-night forage for scones was revealed in the dribble of crumbs on the bare floor around them, and the excitement of the glittering panorama and chaos unfolding beneath them meant that sleep was a distant concession. The mayhem caused by the barn cats, whether intended or not, needed to be addressed. After hearing the unmistakable giggles, she knew who the culprits were.

All three of them sprang up and ran towards her. "Arie!" shrieked Amethyst with delight, exuberantly plastering herself against the soiled gown. She carefully removed the youngest girl's arms and leveled what she hoped was her sternest, most reproving look at Pearl and Ruby.

"What do you have to say for yourselves?"

Ruby clasped her hands behind her and shuffled to and fro on suddenly restless feet. The girl fluttered her lashes so rapidly, Arie feared she'd run through a swarm of gnats. The innocent ploy did not fool her in the least. "I want an explanation, Ruby. Your mischief could've seriously injured some of the guests."

She hung her head. "We didn't think of the consequences," her humbled voice emerged in a croak. "We just wanted to cuddle the cats because our foot warmers had grown cold."

"And you thought bringing the cats in from the barn was a better solution than raising your nurse and asking her to fetch your bottles and rewarm them?" She asked in disbelief. "How'd the cats get into the house?" Arie crossed her arms over her chest and resumed her piercing gaze.

"Jem the stableboy is sweet on Ruby. He'd do anything she asked," Pearl volunteered. "And the cats followed us down to the kitchens when we went to fetch the scones. One of the hounds was sleeping in front of the hearth and the mouser woke him up."

"The mouser just wanted to play!" Amethyst interjected.

"When they went galloping down the hallway, we were scared to go after them," confessed Ruby.

Arie wanted to shake the falsely apologetic, slightly belligerent thirteen-year-old girl standing in front of her. If anyone found out but the four of them that Jem had orchestrated the barn cat invasion, he'd be sacked. Arie knew his widowed mother and five sisters depended on his wages to keep them from going to the workhouse and she suspected Ruby knew it too. "We've spoken before about using your position to manipulate others, Ruby," she admonished.

Ruby raised her head, a flush on her cheeks and dark eyes blazing like Roman candles. "I'd never let anything happen to Jem," she fiercely insisted with clenched fists.

So that was the way the wind was blowing. Apparently Jem's infatuation was not one-sided. Although she didn't believe in the strict social barriers imposed by her son-in-law and his wife, she knew what the consequences would be if the deception and collusion were discovered. Jem would bear the full brunt of the punishment and run the risk of ending up in the workhouse or worse with his family.

"If this conspiracy is discovered, Jem will be the one to pay the price."

This pronouncement upset Ruby even more. "I know!" she wailed, and threw her arms around Arie's waist, oblivious to the odor, her body wracked by sobs. Her tears vigorously soaked the already soiled shoulder of the dress.

"I shall think of another way to explain it," she reassured the girl as she rubbed circles on her back. "As for you, two..." she directed her attention to Pearl and Amethyst. "Does your nurse know you are yet to be abed?"

"No. She won't care. She doesn't care what we do. She thinks we're a bother because we keep her from flirting with the new footman." Pearl confidently asserted.

"I'm sure she cares inasmuch as she wants to keep her job," Arie sarcastically observed. She resolved to speak with the woman about appropriate behavior and remind her of her purpose in the household. "And I'll care if you aren't in top form for your lessons tomorrow morning. If I promise a trip to see the new puppies after we've finished conjugating French, will you seek your beds?"

This proposed bargain was met with shining eyes and clasped hands. Amy, ever shy and quiet, looked up with desperate longing, "Yes, please!"

"Follow me, darlings."

Once the ragamuffins were tangled beneath a mound of blankets, Arie decided it was her turn to seek some comfort. After the chaos dissolved, all Arie could think about was the fact she'd been nearly propositioned by the towering farmer.

The barn was always warm and welcoming, and she knew she would find no judgment or censure there. So she stripped out of her ruined dress, slipped on her wool nightgown, her wrapper, her scarf, and her scuffed half-boots, and escaped to her favorite place.

When Arie ducked into the covered paddocks, the scent of warm hay enveloped her. She took a glorious sniff, and let it settle over her senses. Here always felt like home because she was always enough. The horses and the cows and the cantankerous barn cats didn't care that she was a wainwright's daughter and the widowed third wife.

Here there was no one to point fingers and mutter behind their hands that Araminta Wainwright Greaves' father bartered her away when she was twenty-six in exchange for one of her impeccably trained herder collies.

The irony of the fact that Arie had been the one to hone the dog's herding abilities didn't escape her. Sadie's herding abilities, and the accolades they won her at the county fair, were what sealed her fate.

The late squire had been awed by Sadie's prowess at keeping wayward sheep in line and decided that only she would do as the protector of his new herd of Devon Longwools. When he'd seen Araminta bent over the paddock door, he'd wanted her too. A compliment regarding her luscious rump had been made aloud to her father, and she'd never felt more like an object.

Her father had taken advantage of the squire's fascination and the price of her freedom was the ten-year lease on a mill he'd been coveting. He made a deal with the squire to obtain it. If the man wanted the collie, he'd take the daughter too. And he'd give the wainwright the lease in return. Her closest companion should have been a sufficient trading commodity, but her father hadn't thought twice about throwing Arie in too as an added inducement to sweeten the pot and ensure a deal was struck.

The deal was not in Arie's favor.

The squire was at least three and a half times her age, always smelled like liver and onions because he requested them for every meal, was an ardent admirer of his hunting hounds and allowed them free run of every part of his house, and believed bathing more than once a week would be detrimental to his health. (Which was the most likely explanation for the overwhelming stench of liver and onions.) He acquired things merely for the satisfaction of declaring frequently and loudly that he owned them. Horses. Dogs. Impressionist paintings. Greek statuary. Wives.

Marriage to the squire was only one obstacle in a line of hurdles so long it stretched interminably as far as she could see and obliterated everything but the tiniest spark of hope. She'd trudged wearily through her bondage, and wondered if she'd ever known anything but strife, challenge and struggle.

None of those things were synonymous with happiness and she had no idea how to channel them into some sort of contentment. Once upon a time, a very long time ago, she'd been a barefoot, tousled, carefree girl running amok in the village, and she'd had no trouble finding her joy. But now, after she'd borne the weight of the years, and the wounds they inflicted lay across her shoulders, she'd forgotten how to find it or keep it.

In the fourteen years between her mother's death and her marriage, Arie devoted herself to raising her six younger sisters, ensuring the household ran smoothly, and training the border collies she loved. She became the boring one bound by duty and protocol. She didn't have time to wallow in what could have been or what should be. Every spare minute she had was spent easing the lives of others. She'd always bowed to duty and familial expectation in the hope that eventually all those years of sacrifice would be rewarded when her husband died, and she gained her independence. Then she could thumb her nose at expectations because she wouldn't depend on them for her survival.

As she settled into the bed of straw, she mused on how she'd watched others find happiness and keep it. She wondered if their lives had been less characterized by tragedy and disillusionment. She wondered if they ever went through life with the pervasive, grim determination that forced her to rise from her bed every morning and focus on putting one foot in front of the other. Because if she didn't the weight of her despair would crush her.

Training the dogs was the only peace she carved out for herself, and she continued to do it even after her marriage. Her grandfather had shown her every technique he knew and she'd used them all to cement a reputation as one of the best trainers in Cumbria.

When her burdensome spouse finally keeled over after ten years of marriage, she was relieved. Until she discovered there was no provision for her in his will and she was in dire straits. The solicitor reading the terms aloud had cast her a pitying glance at the end because she was so much of an afterthought she wasn't even mentioned. She was distraught for more lives than her own. She'd lost her chance at independence and the sacrifices she'd made seemed pointless, but she'd intended to rectify wrongs with part of her widow's portion.

She'd succumbed to a rare bout of tears and confessed to her stepson Hugh she'd planned to use the bequest to provide each of her full sisters with a respectable husband who didn't have a reputation as a liar, a cheat or a drunken lout, and a nest egg of fifty pounds upon their marriage. She didn't want them to become casualties of her father's greed. She wanted them to have a choice, so they could marry for love and not survival or convenience. All her sisters but Cecily had remained spinsters.

Never a man to miss an opportunity, her stepson had taken pity on her and extracted a promise in return – her surveillance and care of his three irrepressible daughters in exchange for dowries for her sisters. For the last two years she'd been an unpaid governess to the exuberant girls and an unsung housekeeper because his wife couldn't be bothered to converse with those she considered her social inferiors. In return for three years of her coerced servitude, he'd agreed to provide each of her sisters with a dowry of fifty pounds.

She bore the scorn of Hugh and his wife, Violet, because she didn't want her sisters relegated to a situation like hers. She knew they called her "the Crow" when her back was turned. She knew they did it with no remorse because they knew she'd do nothing to jeopardize the future of her sisters. While Arie cringed at the sting of their disdain and ill humor, she bit her tongue and resigned herself to it. Because they may as well have bent her over a barrel of ale. If she wanted to make sure her sisters didn't suffer a similar fate, she was completely at their mercy.

Since becoming a widow, she'd squeezed her hopes into the rigidity of her diminished role. Even though she knew it did her no favors, she dreamt about how things might have been different. It only made the longing for something else prick more deeply. So she abandoned her dreams and embraced pragmatism.

She lifted a silky pile of puppy into her arms and nuzzled the soft fur behind its ears. Her thoughts flitted briefly to the farmer. He'd been handsome, if oddly out of place. His plain dress and large form were enticing, and she'd noticed them even though she was annoyed at his interruption. She wondered what it would be like to receive his amorous attention.

She'd been subjected to a marriage that meant she was at the beck and call of someone who didn't value her as anything other than a receptacle for his perfunctory, amorous attention.

For ten years, she'd borne his determined plowing. Her failure to thicken with child didn't bother her portly, obstreperous spouse because he had grown children aplenty. When the squire finally keeled over in the saddle in the middle of a fox hunt at the ripe old age of ninety-four, everyone had been surprised. He was so vigorous they'd expected him to outlive them all. Arie just thanked her stars he'd toppled head over heels between his horse's ears instead of expiring while he was huffing and puffing on top of her.

Her marriage had not been a happy one. She'd occupied an isolated, silent sphere – tolerated, but not cherished. An object of convenience to be fed and clothed. The squire had once comforted her by assuring her he didn't mind her infertility because she was such a satisfying depository for his seed. Arie hadn't considered such praise a compliment.

Now that she was widowed, her position was even more precarious. She knew her husband's heir could turn her out on her ear with no means of support. Straight back into the muck of the muddy roads. So she strove to make herself both invisible and invaluable.

She curled her fingers into Sadie's lush coat and stroked the puppy's head. The little man had a dark circle around one eye, like a highway bandit, and had a penchant for snuffling and falling asleep almost immediately. She stroked him as he enthusiastically licked her wrist with his raspy tongue, bathing her forearm, then her elbow. He finally turned around three times in the cramped nest between her knees and nodded off. She knew no one would even notice her absence, so she allowed herself to doze off as well.

She awoke with a start, completely disoriented. She couldn't immediately identify her surroundings and had no idea what time it was. The scent of slightly mildewed hay filled her nostrils, and she reached out to run her fingers through the ruff of the puppy snoring in her lap. The puppy was no longer in her lap, and through a gaze slitted with sleep she observed he was over in the corner tousling with his brothers and sisters. As she fully roused, she swiftly realized she wasn't leaning against the rough boards of the stable wall. Instead, her cheek was resting against something warm and solid. She blinked warily and pushed away. With a flush, she acknowledged she'd been reclining against a very broad chest, and that impossibly long, muscled legs were stretched out in front of her.

Holding a Moonbeam in His Hand

"Who are you? Where am I?" Arie demanded to disguise her alarm. And how flustered the warmth at her back was making her. And how being cradled was kindling a spark of warmth she hadn't felt in eons.

Her demand was met with a throaty chuckle that rumbled up from the depths of the sturdy chest behind her. "Begging your pardon for this unorthodox encounter," a voice like the rush of water over stones in the stream answered. "I dared to impugn you for a dance earlier. My invitation ended abruptly when you insisted you were immune to flattery, shoved a half-full cup of punch into my hands and dove into the fray."

"You were keen to know my inclination to climb trees and my aptitude for fishing," she replied. The oddity of his questions and the way he'd leaned in to hear her answers, had made an indelible impression. It was him. Apparently her rebuff hadn't scared him away forever.

"And don't forget the nature of your hugs. Although after having you sprawled and relaxed over me for the last two hours, I have a fair idea of them. We were introduced at your wedding nearly twelve years ago, but I doubt you recall our meeting. I approached you at the party to renew our acquaintance and I'm here now because you were in danger of planting your face in the muck, and I gallantly swooped to the rescue. Your very own knight in shining armor. Earlier, I was on the precipice of sweeping you into a waltz. We were interrupted by the Tannenbaum disaster. Thaddeus St. Simon at your service."

So she was leaning against the towering farmer who'd nearly propositioned her. His voice had the distinctive cant of Cumbria in it, with the hint of a lilt. He was likely a member of the parish, not a guest attending the fete from far flung locales. She didn't recall seeing him at her wedding, but she'd been wallowing in misery. She snorted. "Although I remember our unfortunate recent meeting, I don't recall being introduced to you at my wedding. I can't say for certain whether you're a knight or a gargoyle. How am I to know what your true intentions are?"

He chuckled again. "I can vouch for my humanity and despite appearances to the contrary, my intentions are honorable. Although the men who served under my command would say I resembled a gargoyle as well."

"As long as you're not that manufactured creature from Shelley and don't possess fangs like the one conjured by Stoker. But you still acted very presumptuously. What if I had a dagger strapped to my thigh and decided stabbing was a better course of action than asking questions?" She wished she had the resources to procure a dagger. It would be the perfect deterrent to lechers and rapscallions. Although technically he didn't fit neatly into either category. Because her skirts were still intact and he wasn't making any sudden, suspect moves.

"Do you have a dagger strapped to your thigh?" He sounded far too intrigued by the notion.

"No. But now I think maybe I should begin resorting to such measures," she ominously replied. "In truth, I spent my entire wedding day numb with disbelief, like a mummy emerging from a sarcophagus. Even if I was introduced to you, it's highly unlikely I'd remember you." He grimaced and she decided she should respond with more grace since he'd apparently rescued her. It seemed unlikely he had nefarious intentions. "You have my sincere gratitude for serving as my make-do pillow."

"After the tree disaster, I escaped the party. Easing a path through the guests congregating in the music room left me no elbow room or air to breathe," he explained. "Even the library and parlor were infernally congested. Too much cloying perfume disguising unwashed bodies and too many voices vying for the award of loudest and most obnoxious. Since I returned from the war, being around that many people at once makes my lungs constrict and my skin itch. I came across you curled up in this empty stall and realized I wasn't the only one keen for escape." He stood and reached for her hand. "Let us move closer to the light so we may become reacquainted."

She slid her hand into a calloused grip, and he effortlessly pulled her upright. She came to the middle of that solid wall of chest and was suddenly acutely aware of the fact she was swanning about in nothing more than her nightclothes, much darned stockings, half boots, and a ragged pashmina shawl. Even if her night rail was a shapeless, flannel monstrosity that buttoned all the way to her throat, and was anything but flattering or revealing, she was still without the armor of petticoats or a shift.

She was in her second year of mourning and had the gray gown in need of reinforcement at the seams, the black bombazine now covered in oyster slime and blood, a navy-blue serge and a scratchy black wool dress to her name. This sharp reminder of her situation did not improve her mood. Her wardrobe was far from flush, but she did everything in her power to ensure she was at least presentable if not in the first stare of fashion. But she was conversing with a guest while she sported a muddy hem and nightclothes that were threadbare around her wrists and beneath her arms.

Because of tonight's fiasco and the antics of the hound last week, her wardrobe was the epitome of deplorable. If she needed an additional gown before her stepson's chokehold on the household purse strings deemed it necessary, she'd be forced to rip down the ugly green paisley drapes in her bedroom and industriously ply her needle by candlelight.

"A gentleman would've woken me up rather than pulling me into his lap." She knew he'd probably saved her from a sneezing fit and an even filthier set of nightclothes, but he was an easy target for her frustration, and she couldn't restrain herself from lashing out.

He gazed steadily at the tilt of her face in the shadowy barn. She wondered how much straw had made its way into her hair. "And what makes you think I'm a gentleman?" he murmured as his mouth curved into one of the rowdiest grins she'd ever seen.

His voice held a husky, teasing note that made her breath catch -as if she was too tightly laced into one of the corsets she stubbornly refused to torture herself with. "I still have my nightclothes on. If you were a villain instead of a gentleman, you would've divested me of them instead of giving me a comfortable place to sleep," she pointed out with asperity. He might not be a gentleman by birth, but if he was truly a scoundrel, she doubted she'd still be swaddled in flannel.

He shrugged. "Mayhap not quite a villain, but not a gentleman either. I'll admit to thoroughly enjoying the feel of your curves against me, even if anyone seeing you at this moment in your gown and wrapper could mistake you for a wraith floating across the moors. Especially silhouetted by moonlight," he observed with another roguish grin.

Her gaze flicked to his bared forearms. They'd been cradling her in a bed of straw a moment ago. She hoped she hadn't drooled on them in her sleep. She wondered if he felt the cold seeping into the barn as keenly as she did. There'd been a nip in the air before the sun disappeared, and now the night was even more frigid, settling around them like a damp shroud. She pulled her shawl more firmly around her shoulders. Both to protect her modesty and ward off the chill creeping up beneath her hem now she wasn't reclining against a human furnace. "You're altogether too sure of yourself," she chastised, unwilling to divulge how much she was enjoying their banter.

He shrugged. "So I've been told. I blame it on my time in the ranks. When death is constantly lurking around every corner speaking anything other than the truth and refusing to enjoy levity at every available opportunity seems a waste of time."

His response was glib and matter of fact. "I haven't heard of your courageous exploits over dinner," she observed. His soldiering didn't completely explain the self-assurance he wore like a mantle across the monumental shelf of his shoulders. She wondered if he'd been an officer.

"I was a captain in the 5th Dragoon Guards. We were repeatedly on the front lines of battle, in the thick of it. And now I use those skills to rescue damsels in distress," he flexed at the waist, bowing with a flourish.

So his air of command was legitimately earned. "Your return to the parish probably irked my stepson. He never mentioned you or even alluded to you. I find that curious since you have one of the largest holdings in the parish."

His mouth tipped into a smile at her revelation. "He wouldn't. He can be obscenely petty at times."

She didn't bother hiding her derisive snort. "Yes, he was probably anything but pleased at your return. I'm quite sure he considers you a disrespectful upstart and affront to good manners."

He shook his head in bemusement. "I'm sure my return was an unwelcome surprise and he's likely been in a pique over it. We've been rivals since I played on the opposing cricket team that trounced him and his cronies. And I was always quicker on my feet with sums, which he didn't appreciate. Especially since it's helped me build quite the nest egg courtesy of railroad investments."

"Yes, he can't stand being second best at anything. Though you'd think he'd be used to it by now. He has a very distorted opinion of himself."

They shared rueful smiles.

"If I remember correctly, the 5th Dragoons were at Balaclava. And since you survived, you likely received a Victoria Cross for your service."

Even beneath the dimly lit eaves of the barn, she could discern his suddenly bereft expression. His grin disappeared and he swallowed. "I was," he confirmed. "And I did."

"I read it was a bloodbath of epic proportions," she laid a hand on his forearm, the urge to offer some small form of comfort and acknowledgment of his sacrifice, impossible to quell. "I'm sorry for the suffering you were forced to endure and grateful for your service to our country." She wondered if he was prey to the night terrors she'd heard many of the veterans suffered from. She imagined the horrors he'd witnessed made finding sleep difficult. She knew firsthand that making the mind bend to restful contemplation was hard when memories were full of images one wished to forget.

The harsh bark of his laughter echoed around them. "A bloodbath is one way to describe it," he raked his hand through his hair. "And not an exaggeration," he clarified. "I'd also call it an unmitigated disaster, a warning against putting fools in leadership positions, and a resounding slap in the face to men far more capable of waging war but held back by the rigid classism of the British army. I've studied all methods of Eastern meditation to lay my memories to rest."

"And yet you survived it," she reminded him. Battlefield heroes were feted when they returned home, and she knew he likely never lacked someone willing to put a pint in his hand at the village tavern. His notoriety had obviously been earned, and Hugh's lack of mention regarding his feats of courage was unsurprising. Anyone that detracted from her stepson's inflated sense of self was only worthy of derision in the Greaves household.

She decided she would ask the housekeeper, Mrs. Rowe, at first opportunity, for more details about her new acquaintance.

"All glory for the feat of my survival goes to my mount, Rampage," he self-consciously ran a hand through his dark hair again and set a long strand loose from his queue. It dangled across his cheek when he shook his head, like one of Medusa's snakes warning anyone who looked at him too closely they'd never be the same. That they'd welcome being turned to stone to avoid the reverberations he'd leave in his wake. "I was fortunate to have such a brave, loyal mount when so many of my compatriots perished."

"Is he here?" she eagerly asked. She'd never had the privilege of seeing one of the celebrated destriers up close and would love to stroke his muzzle, give him an apple, and thank him for keeping this man she barely knew safe from enemy fire and swords. She had a soft spot for fearless horses and brave men.

"No, he's at stud in Sussex. I sold him when I returned to England because I needed the funds to purchase farming equipment while I waited on the returns from some of my investments."

"Are your holdings substantial, then?"

"I'm the second largest landowner in the county." He proudly informed her. "My property directly adjoins your late husband's, ma'am."

The size of his holdings also explained her stepson's covetous need to acquire them and his smoldering animosity. Hugh wanted to be the undisputed biggest fish in the sea. As if Thaddeus's initial purchase hadn't been enough effrontery, he continued to acquire property. "You may call me Arie like everyone else." she frowned at him. "Being addressed as ma'am makes me feel dusty and dowdy and I've always loathed the weight of my full given name."

"We can't have that, Arie," he flashed her another wry grin and she couldn't help noticing the dimple that bracketed the right side of his mouth. "You're too beautiful to ever feel dowdy." The flash of that dimple, and the appreciative gleam in his eyes, incited a blush that suffused her cheeks and throat. She felt anything but dusty and dowdy.

"What do you raise?" She asked trying in vain to ignore the singular allure of that dimple.

"I raise three breeds of sheep -Rough Fells, Herdwicks and Devons. Just as your late husband, Squire Greaves did. But I'm also trying my hand at breeding good plow stock."

"What sort of plow stock? I thought most farmers around here used ponies for everything."

"It's true that the moor ponies are well-suited to the terrain and have been indefatigable in their assistance at the mines. But their smaller size means the amount of acreage they can cultivate in a day is limited. There are some farmers in Suffolk who breed a light draft horse that's strong, yet compact. The breed has been touted as ideal for small farms because its size means it costs less to feed and house. Its sure footing makes it ideal for the hill farming we do here in Cumbria. I have my first batch of yearlings in training, and six of my mares will foal in the spring."

"I'd love to see them," Arie confessed. She loved foals almost as much as she loved puppies. The gangling awkwardness and satiny soft muzzles were the perfect reminder of spring. "You never told me how you ended up in the barn," she prodded. "Did you hear my loquacious stepson bragging about the litter of puppies?" She narrowed her eyes at him. Hugh bragged incessantly about the pedigree of Sadie's whelp. And once he sold them he never bothered to share the profits with her.

"I did not. I was determined to leave after the disaster and came out here to saddle my mount."

"That was hours ago, wasn't it?"

"Yes. When I went to tighten the girth, I noticed he was favoring his front left foreleg."

Her eyes widened in alarm. "Is he well?"

"Yes, just a rock I dislodged. It bruised him, though. I'll need to borrow a mount to get home. I was going to notify the head grooms-man when I heard you snuffling in your sleep. My plans didn't extend beyond preventing you from taking your rest on the hard floor. Now that you're awake, I'd best be on my way. It's nearly dawn."

"You aren't staying for the entire four days of festivities?" She tried to hide her disappointment.

"No," Thaddeus tersely replied, shaking his head. "I am not a man of leisure and I have four maids at home I cannot long ignore."

"Four maids?" her brow furled in confusion.

"My very inquisitive, very independent daughters."

A knot of tangled disappointment lodged in her chest and she cupped her hand against her heart. "And you should return home to your wife as well."

He pulled her hand loose, clasping it in his giant palm, swallowing it as his thumb slid across her knuckles. He gave her a measuring look. "I often crave rational conversation because I receive none at home. Even my eldest, Clementine, can drive one mad with her endless rounds of questions and the other three frequently confound me with their refusal to eat beans one day and turnips the next."

"It sounds like they keep you and your wife quite busy. It's good you have each other to provide more mature discussion." The knowledge of his marriage was just another spoke in the interminable wheel of her humdrum life. She needed to immediately bury the irrational glimmer of disillusionment that had flickered to life in her gut. There was no reason for it because the last thing she needed was entanglement. Especially the kind involving brawny chested former soldiers who smelled like horse and leather and man. No matter how enticing she found his deep voice or broad shoulders or the scent of sunshine and brimstone that seemed to cling to him.

"I'm a widower, Arie. If I'd still been married I would've gently nudged you awake instead of making the choice to hold you instead," he softly informed her. His expression was somber and full of sorrow. "We had a brood of seven when I left for war, and Rachel was carrying a babe. When I returned from serving in both the Crimea and on the Continent, I'd lost Rachel and my three sons. All were taken by diphtheria but the newborn babe. I don't know how my wee scrap of a daughter managed to survive, but she did. Her sisters and I decided to name her Claire because she brought light into our lives when we desperately needed it."

Arie was stricken by the depth of sadness that carved his features. "That must have been hard. Burying your family and comforting your daughters at the same time."

"Aye. I did everything I could, but there were days I couldn't get past the grief and I had to turn to others for help. My parents took the girls in for a time after Rachel's death so I could come to terms with my guilt at chasing glory abroad instead of spending my days making a comfortable home for my family. They still have a hand in the raising of my offspring, although even constant surveillance has proven inadequate where the twins are concerned. Rachel's parents blamed me for the loss – insisting if I'd been there it never would've happened. That my presence would have somehow ensured her survival and that of the rest of our children."

"They wanted you to feel guilty for your survival," she observed.

"Yes. Because war should've been a much more dangerous endeavor than managing a farm and a household in Cumbria."

"I am so sorry for all that you've lost."

He roughly exhaled. "Though my life has been marred by tragedy, my daughters ensure my days are filled with laughter," his eyes grew misty, and he gave her a rueful smile.

She knew she should pull her hand from his grasp, but she was enjoying the brusque caress.

"Your name's very daunting and describes you perfectly," he confided.

"Why would you characterize me as daunting?" She liked to think her name was a perfect expression of the reflection she wanted to see in the mirror. Unfortunately, she rarely had the chance to show her inner mettle because of her social position and obligations. Because her survival was dependent on the mercy and benevolence of others.

Because she must bend to their every whim and grievance if she wanted a roof over her head.

"Because it means both prayer and protection," he murmured, still caressing her hand.

She blushed at his reference to the meaning behind her name, and gingerly extracted her digits from that dangerous caress. From the addictive warmth of that calloused palm and innocuously stroking thumb. She decided to throw him off-kilter. "And you have a courageous heart...or you're a traitor and coward."

His brows rose in surprise. "So you enjoy cataloguing people as well based on their given names?"

She blushed. She wasn't accustomed to sharing her logophile tendencies with people and didn't know why she was compelled to reveal them to him on such short acquaintance. Apparently he had them too. Ah well, in for a penny was in for a pound. "Etymology has always fascinated me. So, yes. There's debate over whether it's another spelling or a reference to Judas, or if it's from the original Aramaic for courageous heart."

She couldn't decipher his gaze, but it seemed to convey both awe and confusion. "You're an unusual woman," he observed.

"So I've been told. When that comment is launched in my direction, it's usually not meant to flatter. Quite the opposite, in fact." She glanced down, her cheeks and throat on fire, the flush spreading across her collarbones. "I'm sorry. That wasn't an appropriate comment, and most certainly not fitting repartee to make on first acquaintance."

He stepped closer. "I wasn't insulted, just caught off guard. That hasn't happened in a very long while. Not since long before I returned home from war," he clarified.

She sensed the reluctance behind his admission. And could see it had surprised him. She set about putting him at ease. "As I said, I don't remember being introduced to you at the wedding, I think my misery obscured everything. I'm sure I would've remembered your height. You probably dwarfed everyone else in the room."

He chuckled. "Aye. I tend to do that. Makes finding my partner, or a hidden alcove, or an escape route, all the easier," his gaze became sympathetic. "But it also made it difficult to do things like swipe pies from windowsills as a lad. I think the entire village knew about the circumstances of your marriage. It can't have been the answer to your dreams to be bartered to a man almost four times your age."

Arie leaned forward and winked conspiratorially. She'd long ago laid her innocent dreams to rest. They were a reminder she could ill afford if she had any hope of resilience. "No. He certainly wasn't my Prince Charming. Maybe my Beast. But not in a good, enchanted fairytale kind of way. More like the odiferous, belching, flatulent kind. The proliferation of hair in his nose and ears needed its own postal address."

He roared with laughter. "That would've been terrifying," his grin faded, and his expression intensified. "Your ability to find humor in what couldn't have been a welcoming situation is admirable." This wasn't simple flattery. It was as if he were admiring something he wanted to emulate, a reaction or an ability he'd been unable to channel himself.

Her answering laugh was tinged with bitterness. "Humor has been the key to my survival. It kept the darkness at bay when life relentlessly crushed every hope you've ever nourished."

His gaze searched hers once again. "The moonlight demands both clarity and honesty from both of us. But you shouldn't be sharing your secrets with a near stranger."

"Who else would I share them with? I seem trapped in this inexorable circle of purgatory, not one thing and not quite another. It's demeaning and soul-destroying and I feel like I'm trapped in an eternal winter of discontent. It's a relief to speak my feelings aloud to an actual person." She wanted to bite her tongue for a confession that surely made him as uncomfortable hearing it as she felt giving it.

"I'm honored to hear them. And as Shakespeare reminds us in Richard III, all the clouds on our house will soon be buried in the ocean." There wasn't a hint of irony in his reply, and she finally relaxed her guard. The tension slid from her shoulders, and she finally accepted his honest intentions.

"I'd love to make the acquaintance of your daughters. My step-granddaughters are in sore need of playmates."

"That might be arranged. So long as you accompany them."

She felt the blush darken her cheeks again. She had the distinct sense he was flirting with her. Even though she'd done absolutely nothing to encourage it. "The pedagogues say the sins of our youth are revisited upon us when we meet our children. Have you found that to be true?"

His smile was swift and bright, a slash of humor with the gleam of teeth and a dimple like a comma bracketing the right side of his mouth. Carefree laughter erupted from him. "My mother would say she is being avenged for all the scrapes and worry and heartache I put her through." He grasped her hand once again, sliding his thumb across her knuckles "Were you serious about making their acquaintance? Their shenanigans can chase away the doldrums on the dreariest of days and I suspect you need cheering. And as I said, I'd love to spend more time in your company."

She nodded shyly. "I think a playdate would do the four of them good," she adroitly deflected. "Although Ruby is not much older than Pearl, she enjoys telling her younger sisters what to do. I'm sure she won't balk at the prospect of additional subjects or the opportunity to discuss frocks and ribbons with your eldest daughter."

"Consider it done. I'll send over a more formal invitation. Perhaps a playdate that includes a pony ride around the paddock for the girls and a sedate promenade through the woods for us?"

"Although the thought of the mischief that could ensue from such a meeting makes me faint of heart, I think it would do them good. They are too much confined to their own company." And if a play date meant she could spend more time with this delicious man, even better. "And I never have the chance to ride, so if a gallop rather than a promenade could be arranged, that would be more to my liking. My stepson didn't see the point of providing room and board for the mount of his father's widow. Fireflower was sold at auction nearly a year ago," she confessed. The loss of her beloved mare had left a gaping hole in her heart.

His expression darkened. "If I'm not mistaken, you provide most, if not all, of the care and instruction to his daughters."

"I have to make certain sacrifices to keep a roof over my head."

"But you shouldn't have to. Your stepson should feel an obligation to your care. It's a matter of honor – especially for one that can well afford it."

Arie slid her hand from the cradle of his, mollified by his thunderous expression. He was outraged on her behalf. He was the first person who'd bothered to express indignation at the lack of provision for her in the squire's will. "Whether or not I agree with your assessment, I simply have no choice in the matter. Everything was entailed, and my husband lacked the foresight for planning anything beyond the next hunt or barrel of port. I was an afterthought," she bitterly surmised.

"You do have a choice, Arie. Your widowhood didn't make you a martyr."

"You don't understand the position I'm in."

"You're wrong. I would offer you a thousand counter arguments and alternative suggestions, but I need to return home. Rest assured we'll continue this conversation when next we meet."

He clasped her arm just above the elbow, his thumb skating over the indent in a subtle caress as he reeled her in. "And mayhap you'll find out how ungentlemanly I can be when I want something very much," he rumbled into the shell of her ear and touched his lips to the upper curve of her cheek and the underside of her wrist.

She tipped her head infinitesimally in response, her stomach rioting at the thought. "I look forward to it."

As she made her way back to her spartan bedroom, she mused over the encounter. There had been both concern and interest in his forthright gaze. She felt strangely enervated, and the ruddy skin of her hand and her cheek were still tingling from the fleeting press of his mouth.

***

Thad watched her walk away, her back ramrod straight. He wondered if the touch of his lips on her skin had affected her as much as it affected him. He didn't know what madness had compelled him to gather her limp figure into his arms. But he hadn't blinked at the risk of discovery. He'd relished the weight of her resting against him, the adorable snuffles she exhaled as she snuggled closer.

He wanted to deepen their acquaintance. He wanted to show her that not all men were beasts who placed women in untenable circumstances. He wanted to show her that a man's touch could take her needs and comfort into consideration – that it wasn't always something to brace oneself against and endure. He'd heard of her deceased husband's proclivity for rutting like a barnyard animal and he highly doubted she'd experienced any pleasure in her marital bed. The old lecher had boasted enough times in the tavern that his much younger wife had brought the best sheep herding dog in three counties to his farm as well as a most savory rump.

He knew some marriages were like a war zone and women were forced into endless forays behind enemy lines. Forays that left emotional scars and gutted self-belief. He could see that Arie Greaves was a wild rose and she needed to bloom beyond the fences hedging her in. That a lifetime of being a commodity and a convenience had made it hard for her to believe anyone had selfless intentions.

Unpredictable as Weather

The next morning, Arie sought out Mrs. Rowe and commented on Hugh's failure to acknowledge the returned war hero. The housekeeper had rolled her eyes. "The vicar tutored Mr. Snootiness and Mr. St. Simon. The physician's boy always got the better of him – in letters and on the cricket field. He bought that farm with money he invested in railroads. Of course Hugh had his eye on it. As you well know, Hugh's one to hold a grudge, and I'm sure he's never forgotten the constant comeuppance he suffered as a lad. And probably thinks St. Simon stole the property right from under his nose."

Still curious, Arie asked the maids about him later that afternoon. They'd all been in raptures. They'd had been a wealth of information about him and insisted he stood head and shoulders above all the other eligible bachelors. He was older, too, but not too old according to the upstairs chamber maid, Louisa. "He's roundabout forty-two, and seasoned, mum," she'd confided to Arie when they were making the beds. "He looks like he knows his way around a woman's body and wouldn't be stintin' with the givin' o' pleasure. There were lots of us chasing after him before he settled down. And afterward too," she confided. That loaded observation, the knowledge that he had a reputation between the sheets, danced through her head as she remembered the flex of his bicep through the thin cotton of his shirt.

The invitation to a light supper and tour of the farm two days hence arrived first thing the next morning. Her heart lit up when she held it to her cheek and beat faster at the thought of seeing him so soon after their meeting in the stable. She'd cynically concluded there would be no invitation forthcoming and resigned herself to that fact.

Hugh glared down at her from his seat at the head of the table. She was ensconced near the end as usual, taking care of Ruby, Pearl, and Amethyst. Her stepson decried that if she was insistent about them taking meals with the adults, it was her responsibility to tend them. Which meant she usually spent the entire meal cutting their food into minuscule pieces or ensuring they didn't somehow sneak unwanted morsels like Brussel sprouts to the hounds.

"Although he's a Crimean veteran, he's not a respectable war hero. He went gallivanting off and left behind his wife and children. And now he's back and trying to get all the landowners to embrace new-fangled farming ideas like using mechanized reapers and winnowers in his fields. He's shown no interest in finding a new Mrs. St. Simon and I've heard rumors in the village that his children run amok. I don't believe it's fitting for my daughters to frolic with a pack of wild heathens. They may be unduly influenced." His observation should've been sarcastic, but he and his wife didn't spend enough time with their offspring to be appraised of the girls' already very pronounced penchant for wreaking havoc. The girls were dear to her, but she wasn't blind to their faults. Especially their heathenish tendencies. She decided the best course of action was to diffuse his aversion and cater to his arrogance.

"They may also be a positive influence on Mr. St. Simon's daughters," she carefully laid the knife and fork beside her plate, nudging Amy to eat the lamb she'd just carved into absurdly tiny pieces.

Hugh snorted. "It rarely works that way."

Violet placed a deceptively solicitous hand on his forearm, her eyes narrowed on Arie. "Perhaps it's a good idea for the girls to stretch their legs. They've been cooped up the last few weeks because of the inclement weather. And Arie's mourning period is nearly over."

What Violet didn't express, but Arie sensed, was her simmering resentment of Arie's presence and her need to blame the obscure widow for last night's debacle. And last night was quite a disaster. At least five guests were groaning into buckets in the upstairs chambers, courtesy of the turned oysters. And after those not heaving up their guts had scurried away from the ballroom for fear of being squashed, the much smaller music room had proven an inadequate alternate venue. Several enterprising young ladies of great ambition but little talent had taken turns at the pianoforte. The hounds had bayed in unison to the barely disguised screeching.

Although Arie had relinquished any outward semblance of control over the running of the household, Violet was miffed at the staff's proclivity to obey any request she made in her gentle tone. Arie had no doubt the wrecked holiday party would be a weapon the woman used against her for years to come.

Violet's frequent histrionics, strident voice and spoiled demeanor didn't inspire loyalty. If anyone asked Arie to describe her stepson's wife, she'd just tell them to imagine Caroline Bingley emerging from the pages of *Pride and Prejudice*, with a beak of a nose that stayed in the air and a constant mien of self-righteous disdain.

The insufferable woman believed the fastest way to ensure she had complete dominion over the household was to rid herself of Arie as fast as possible and decent, by any means necessary. Even if it meant foisting her on a man she barely knew. Apparently Violet thought the widowed soldier was the perfect candidate. Likely due to the fact Hugh hadn't bothered to hide his animosity and if being thrust together had the outcome Violet desired, Arie would be out of sight and out of mind. She wondered if Violet had considered what her absence would mean for her daughters. If Arie was suddenly removed from their presence, the self-absorbed woman would have to take a more active role in their lives. At the very least she'd have to acknowledge their existence long enough to find Arie's replacement.

Arie wasn't angry at the barely veiled attempt at matchmaking. Although she barely knew Thaddeus St. Simon she wanted to explore the tenuous connection that had blossomed between them. Even if it was foolish and ill-advised. Even if by doing so she was playing straight into Violet's hands. "It would be beneficial for the girls to make the acquaintance of what will one day be their local social circle. I am given to understand that Mr. St. Simon's holding is quite substantial."

Arie held her breath and focused on moving the coddled eggs from one side of her plate to the other. She preferred hers scrambled with cream and butter. But her stepson would tolerate no preferences across the dining table but his own.

Thomas huffed. "Yes. His is the next largest property in the parish in terms of acreage. And his herds of sheep are almost as substantial as the estate's. But he purchased it through investments in railroads. I don't approve of his audacity and his indulgence in something that smacks so much of the bourgeois, but you've made your point. Fine. You may accept the invitation." He waved his hand as if he were anointing her with a scepter and promptly gave his full attention to his wife.

Arie sighed in relief. She let her mind wander over the possibility inherent in her next encounter with Thaddeus St. Simon until she was startled from her reverie by a tug on her sleeve. Amethyst gave her pleading eyes the size of saucers. "I can go too?"

Arie braced herself for the impending tantrum. "Amy, you're too young."

The blond cherub's face crumpled, and she flounced dramatically to her floor. Her wails were so strident they echoed from the rafters. The thud of her heels was dulled by the carpet, but her howling reached a gradual crescendo, until the volume eclipsed everything else.

Violet's eyes narrowed and she shot Arie a glare abrasive enough to melt glaciers. "You will take care of this!" She commanded. "My nerves are fraught after the ridiculous melee you caused last night and cannot take any more stimulation like this unbearable fracas!" She waved vaguely toward her prostrate daughter.

Hugh leapt from his chair like it was a nest of hornets and scurried in her wake. The servants, Arie and the girls watched them go with mingled relief and exasperation.

At some point, Arie might claim a life for herself. She wondered at the fate of the girls when she would no longer be a buffer and they would be forced to deal with a mother who clearly considered them a nuisance instead of a blessing. She sighed and picked up the flailing girl.

Amy bracketed her chubby toddler arms around Arie's neck, and exhaled a series of sharp whimpering sobs that vibrated against her shoulder. She rubbed the little girl's lower back in soothing circles. She wasn't going to change her mind about letting her accompany them, but she needed to resolve the child's sense of loneliness and abandonment. Arie was convinced the frequent thrashing and fits of pique were meant to garner the attention of the girls' mother. From what Arie had witnessed in the two years she'd been close enough to Violet to form an opinion, the woman had no use for her daughters.

They weren't boys and because they didn't serve what she deemed to be a useful purpose; she chose to ignore their existence.

Because Arie had her own experience of parental apathy, she empathized with the Greaves offspring. Unfortunately, there was little she could do. She'd need to ensure that the nursemaid was able to dote on Amy in her absence.

She rose from the table with sudden alacrity, even with Amy clinging to her, eager to tie up all the loose ends and pen her acceptance for the invitation three days hence. She'd make her weekly visit with her sisters and she and the girls would set off when she returned.

***

Thaddeus had scribbled out the invitation the previous night almost immediately after he'd crossed his own threshold. He hadn't been able to banish the image of her uplifted face in the dim light of the barn.

For the first time in years, his dreams hadn't been full of blood and gore and screaming. He hadn't woken up shivering in cold sweat. Instead, he'd vividly dreamt of the warm weight of Araminta Greaves sprawled across his lap in a bed of straw. Of unwrapping her one obstructive, maddening layer of clothing at a time. Of kissing the delicate bones of her ankles, sliding his lips across her calves and the satiny clasp of her thighs. He'd seen her lashes flutter, almost imperceptibly, when he'd kissed her wrist and didn't think his fascination was one-sided. He dared to hope she'd accept the invitation. The thought of those lashes fluttering against his thigh had made his cock hard and aching.

LONGING FOR ADVENTURE

Arie's father had wed the chandler's widow as soon as he'd pawned Arie on Squire Greaves. The entire village had been agog when he'd confessed his adultery in front of the entire congregation and the chandler's impotence had become common knowledge. After providing enough fodder for the village gossip for the next three decades, he'd promptly asked the chandler's widow to marry him. Ostensibly so he could help her raise their two daughters. He lavished all his attention on his newly acknowledged family and ignored the needs of Arie's sisters. They complained to Arie that they all felt like Cinderella covered in soot and ashes and wearing sackcloth. Arie had spent the last ten years doing what she could to mitigate their situation. When the squire was alive and she was tasked with maintaining the household accounts, she'd always been able to order a spare bolt of cloth here and there and send weekly provisions. Since her miserly stepson had inherited the estate, her largesse was limited to the occasional loaf of bread and jar of jam.

"I appreciate the bread and the jam, but you can visit us without bearing gifts. We don't expect it Arie. You've no reason to feel you have to ingratiate yourself or take care of us," Cecily admonished as she took the basket Arie proffered. "We're no longer merely your younger siblings in need of coddling and protection."

"I know, but I feel guilty because we have so much and I fear my sisters are not being provided for."

"We manage to scrape by, Arie." Lavinia's eyes twinkled up at her from her position on the settee.

Arie shrugged as she seated herself beside her sister. "That may be so. But why not supplement where you can? Especially when they won't even notice it's gone amidst all the holiday baking. After three full nights of buffoonery, the guests were still snoring in their beds when I crept away."

"You usually visit us in the middle of the week, not so near the beginning. And you're a creature of routine, Big Sister. Why the deviation?"

Arie flushed. "I have a confession."

Both of her sisters eagerly leaned forward.

When she remained silent, Lavinia raised a brow. "I'm ever so glad I have an hour for my lunch, because it may take that long for you to gather enough courage to spill your secrets and tell us why you changed your schedule."

Lavinia apprenticed with the elderly village apothecary. It wasn't a profession often occupied by women, but the man had also been one of the natural sciences teachers at the parish school. He'd been so impressed by her aptitude for chemistry, he'd asked her to consider becoming his apprentice when she turned sixteen. According to Lavinia, despite his dour expression he was more of a father to her than theirs had ever been.

"I think I may have a potential suitor."

Cecily bounced from her chair and gleefully clapped her hands. "Did you meet someone at the ball? I heard about the disaster! If you did, at least some good came out of it."

"Who is this mysterious gentleman, Arie?" Prompted Lavinia.

"His name is Thaddeus St. Simon."

Cecily's eyes widened. "He is much sought after and seldom landed. The single women in my charity sewing circle, and even some of the married ones, have admitted they'd take him on in the space of a heartbeat for the sake of his thighs alone."

"Did you notice his thighs, Arie?" Lavinia mischievously asked.

There was a clatter outside and Gertrude came through the door. "What's this about strapping thighs?" She demanded as she hung her cloak on the peg.

"Arie met Thaddeus St. Simon."

"Ooh! He definitely has strapping thighs. The perfect epitome of a Gothic hero carrying a heroine across the windswept moors after she's turned her ankle." Gertrude, or Gertie as her sisters called her, managed the town's circulating library, and had a fondness for angst-filled books with ghosts, lost inheritances, and mysterious quests.

"Vinia, you're incorrigible. You asked inappropriate questions when you were twelve as well. But it was hard not to notice his thighs," she paused for effect before continuing. "Especially considering I woke up splayed across them."

"You had a tryst?" Squealed Ceci.

"No, I didn't have a tryst," Arie primly informed her.

"Then how on earth did you end up in his lap?" Demanded Gertie.

Arie blushed again. The whole meeting sounded so incongruous and foolish now. "I went to the stable to check on Sadie's latest litter and fell asleep in one of the stalls. He apparently swooped in to prevent me from getting mud on my face and straw in my hair."

"So he rescued you from ignominy at least," surmised Gertie. "That's certainly something a hero would do. At least he didn't do something dastardly."

Vinia frowned. "If he'd hurt you or importuned you, I would've found a way to poison him. He has a standing order for liniment and there are a lot of enhancements I could make that would give him a rash."

Arie shook her head, amused by her sister's vehemence. "He did neither. He was the consummate gentleman. Even though he assured me he was far from it."

"He told you he wasn't a gentleman? What exactly did he say?"

"He told me he wasn't quite a villain, but he wasn't a gentleman either. He said he thoroughly enjoyed the feel of my curves against him and wouldn't mind showing me exactly how ungentlemanly he could be."

Cecily gasped in delight. "Oh my. I think I just swooned."

"According to the upstairs maids, he tends to have that effect."

"Color me intrigued."

"I'm intrigued as well, Vinia. I won't deny it. But I shouldn't be. It's imprudent."

"You've been prudent your entire life, Arie. And for what? Prudence has brought you nothing but misery," Gertie caustically observed.

"Prudence was what put meals on the table and clothes on your back when our father was either oblivious or sneaking around with the chandler's wife."

"There's no cause to take the high road, Arie," Cecily gently chided. "We want you to be happy. We want you to stop making unnecessary sacrifices on our behalf."

"I refuse to argue about this. I've seen what happens to women who have no choices."

"Arie," Cecily gave her a stern look. "Even though you're the eldest, sometimes you can be the most obtuse. Your sacrifice ensured we all have choices. When are you going to realize you can finally put yourself first?"

Gertrude halted beside her chair and placed a gentle hand on her shoulder. "Cici has the right of it. We're fine Arie. We've been reassuring you for the last four years, and it hasn't sunk in. We make do and manage to put food on the table. Honestly, our wardrobe seems to be in better shape than yours." She cast a disapproving glance over Arie's bedraggled, nearly threadbare gown. "Frances is helping with a labor and delivery, but we know she's likely the only one of us you'll listen to. Be prepared to listen to her lecture the next time you visit."

Despite her sisters' reassurances, Arie was determined to ensure their futures were secured. "I'll not shirk my responsibility."

All three of them shook their heads at her determined tone.

"You were the one that kept us together after Mother died. You made certain we had food in our bellies and shoes on our feet. When are you going to let go and realize we're all grown up and responsible for our own choices?" Lavinia demanded.

"I made a promise." Arie mutinously insisted.

Gertrude threw her hands in the air. "There's no reasoning with you! We want you to be happy, Arie. You deserve it. The promise you made has been fulfilled. You taught us to stand up for ourselves and what we want, and nothing has served us better."

"Arie," Cecily knelt in front of her and gently unfurled the hands clasped at her waist. "When Henry died, you made sure I didn't throw myself into the empty grave. When Father cast us aside like orphans to settle in with his new family, you didn't abandon us. You are always the one who gives and never the one who receives. It has to end." Her eyes sparkled with tears and sudden mischief. "Find a way to indulge your curiosity about that man's thighs."

Arie closed her eyes against their onslaught. She didn't know how to be anyone other than who she was. The one who picked up the pieces. The one who intimately knew the trick of bending without breaking. "I'm afraid." She confessed.

"We know, Arie." Cecily's intent gaze was full of sympathy. "You don't trust yourself to let go. You don't see yourself the way we see you."

"You can be happy, Arie. We don't know what that looks like for you, but if the first step to finding it is Thaddeus St. Simon's thighs, then sobeit." Lavinia's gaze was earnest as well.

Arie was the eldest. She'd always been the one with the insightful pronouncements and encouragement. "I just want to protect you," she murmured.

"We appreciate everything you've done for us. But we can make our own way now. We just want our sister to be happy too." Getrude assured her.

"I'm afraid I'll have to figure out how to do that."

As she made her way back to the manor, the empty basket swinging on her arm, she didn't feel the chill on her cheeks. Her sisters' admonitions were running riot through her thoughts, and she didn't know what to do with them. Her presence at the manor hinged on the bargain she'd made – if her sisters refused to accept the fruits of that bargain, where did that leave her?

***

If Arie was making the journey to the St. Simon farm alone, she'd be walking. She loved traipsing across the moors, even when the sky was violet and ominous, and the wind whipped her clothes around her with so much vigor her sleeves could be wings. But she didn't want her charges for the day to be exhausted before the adventure even began. Hugh had felt the need to lecture her for over an hour on proper behavior, how he expected his daughters to comport themselves and how she must keep the incorrigible and unsavory Thaddeus St. Simon at arms' length. They were off to a delayed start because of the unexpected interruption, and Arie couldn't help glancing at the darkening sky with a furrowed brow. The clouds had a heavy weighted look that heralded snow.

She'd requested one of the light carriages be hitched to the dray horses. The rain had been nothing more than a light mist when they left the manor. And then the steel gray clouds hanging low on the horizon opened up. The light mist became a torrent. And then a slushy mix of droplets and snowflakes.

They were toggling along at a fairly rapid pace when the carriage lurched to the side. The driver's shouts flew back to them, rising over the wind, as he sawed at the reins. When they came to a shuddering stop, it was eerily silent, and the girls had her hands in a death grip. The driver swung the door open, "A cardinal spooked one of the horses, ma'am, and now one of the wheels is stuck fast in the mud. We're closer to our destination than the manor, so I'm setting off on foot to get assistance. I'm leaving a pistol with Jem so he can keep an eye out until we return."

"Thank you, Tobias. I'll keep the girls inside the carriage and wait for rescue," she gave Ruby a pointed look. The fact that her crush was left to guard them did not mean she'd allow her out of the carriage.

Arie occupied the girls with a game of impromptu I Spy that Ruby very obviously felt she was too advanced for. After a quarter of an hour, they ran out of things to describe and both girls began complaining about the encroaching cold and lack of movement. She was relieved beyond words when she heard the clatter of hooves.

Before she'd finished bundling the girls up, Thaddeus wrenched open the door with wild eyes and flushed cheeks. She'd swear on Violet's vial of hartshorn he was on the verge of unceremoniously hauling her into his arms. "Thank goodness the three of you are safe," he murmured, as he dove forward and settled for placing a swift kiss on Arie's forehead. She was so stunned by his passionate declaration she didn't reel back.

It was the first time she'd seen him in full daylight. His eyes were so light green they were nearly chartreuse, and he wore his hair too long for fashion. His temples were streaked with white, and when he leaned toward her the sharp sunlight threw the scar that curved along his cheek into harsh relief. It pulled one corner of his mouth up in a perpetual smirk that was an unsurprising echo of the independent spirit she'd only glimpsed in the stable. His size and his scars should have been imposing in the daylight. She should have felt like an oarless canoe adrift on perilous waters. Instead, the promise of his strength drew her in like a beacon. Offering a bulwark against the threat of rocky shoals. She'd bet those shoulders were capable of sheltering those he loved from any storm.

As soon as he ducked from view, the girls turned to her in wide-eyed astonishment. "Arie, who is that?" demanded Ruby.

"And why did he kiss your forehead?" demanded Pearl, her brows scrunched together in suspicion.

"Mr. St. Simon owns the neighboring farm that is our destination. His daughters are the young ladies I hope you will soon call playmates and friends."

"That still doesn't explain the forehead kiss," Arie heard Ruby mutter behind her as she eased open the carriage door and stepped down. She couldn't explain the significance of the forehead kiss because she didn't have an explanation. It had been unexpected, but natural. "Girls, stay here while I speak with Mr. St. Simon," she called over her shoulder. When she rounded the carriage, he was crouching low to the ground, one foot braced in the ditch. He and the coachman were attempting to lift the vehicle back onto the road.

He shoved his shoulder against the edge of the wagon, grunted and heaved upward. She could see the muscles flexing in his back and his buttocks. The rippling view made her clench her fists so hard her nails dug into the tender flesh of her palms beneath her gloves. She watched, riveted, as the wheels moved slowly away from the ditch, until all four were once again on solid ground. Thaddeus slowly eased his way up from the crouch. He was nearly vertical again when his boot slid, and he went tumbling into the mud and fell back into the ditch.

He lurched to his feet, laughing uproariously with her coachman. Even though she couldn't see the delectable crinkles that were evidence of his glee, she imagined tracing them with the pads of her fingers. She could see the movement of his Adam's apple as he threw his head back. She couldn't look away from the spectacle he made. Because even though any member of the county landed gentry that saw him in this situation would label him something to be dissected, she didn't see him that way. He was elemental and real and tangible. Those crinkles were laugh lines that told the story of his sorrows and joys. He hadn't reached the space he occupied now unscathed. Those treks were a map of all the obstacles he'd overcome. All the godawful fences he'd straddled and leapt over.

Just as hers were. The acknowledgment of their shared affinity was a powerful motivation. She suspected he would celebrate the remnants of battle that lined her countenance instead of relegating them to the sidelines like an unwanted postilion.

When she'd looked in the mirror after her morning ablutions she'd taken note of the fine lines around the edges of her eyes that became more pronounced when she smiled. She'd seen several gray hairs mixed in with her dark chestnut waves, and her body was considerably rounder than the current fashion. Both her age and her love of sweets had thickened her waist and a corset would never give her a waspish figure, so she refused to subject herself to ignominy. She wore a shift instead, cinched at the waist. She had a generous bosom, a generous rump, thighs that plumped above her stockings, and dimples behind her knees. She liked the comfort of her body and was at home in her skin. His thinly veiled promise to show her just how ungentlemanly he could be meant her abundant curves tempted him. She wanted him to do naughty things to her. Craved it.

His eyes alighted on her, and he raised a brow at her obvious scrutiny. And returned her heated gaze with one of his own, his eyes scaling her body from head to toe in a leisurely perusal. She couldn't disguise the flush stealing over her cheeks or make herself look away. She lifted her chin and decided to disconcert him. She let her eyes rove over him in return. A reciprocal scrutiny that made her toes curl in her boots. She was instantly gratified when his cheeks flushed to match hers.

He strode toward her and caught her hand up in his. She could feel the scorching heat of him even through the leather of his gloves and the scratchy wool of her own. "Please allow me to exert my influence and change your mode of transport to the farm."

"Why? You've managed to extract the carriage from the mud." A rebellious part of her might like the thought of him taking control of her, but she resented him taking control of the situation at hand. She balked because his request sounded more like a command. As much as she wanted to let him engineer everything to his satisfaction, like the soldier he was, she didn't want to wholly surrender her own command.

"Yes, but the snow is accumulating, and the roads will only worsen. It would ease my mind if we took the horses to the house," he insisted.

"There aren't enough mounts for everyone," she pointed out. Did he expect them all to double up? Sharing a mount would be improper. Unwise. Inappropriate. Too tempting by far. The thought of those thighs she'd just seen crouching in the mud bracketing her own nearly stole her breath away.

"If we unhitch your carriage horses, you can ride in front of me on Roland," he proposed, as if he'd been reading her thoughts. "Your coachman can take one of the mounts and lead the girls on the other one."

"It's improper for me to ride with you," she protested. Improper and all those other warnings she should heed instead of accepting his offer. Reckless. Oblivious. Heedless of all warnings to the contrary. Abandoning all trace of common sense and cautious, calibrated up-bringing. Spitting in the face of good judgment.

"Even if it's only to see you safely to your destination?"

"That's the only reason?" she challenged.

His eyes glimmered with banked heat. "I confess my motives aren't completely innocent. Yes, I want to save you from freezing to death in the snow," he confirmed. "But I also want to relish the feel of you in my arms again," he huskily finished.

His fears were justified. Just last year, one of the youngest boys in the Wilson brood had been lost in a late season blizzard. It had been a somber February morning when they'd buried him in the hardened ground of the parish cemetery.

Even though his concerns were justified, the knowledge of that justification didn't detract from the persuasive insistence in his tone.

Even though she'd been craving it, she was flustered by his attention. And she didn't trust his motives. There was clearly attraction between the two of them, but she was wary of being another convenient object for men. Objectification had been the trajectory of her entire life story and she wasn't about to succumb to it again. No matter how intoxicating the surrender looked if you were peering into the shop window and compiling a wish list composed of nothing but impossible things.

Did he seek to insert her into the empty space once occupied by his wife? Did he seek to supplant those memories with a warm body that was ideally situated to mother his daughters because she had only bleak prospects? Did he secretly pity her? No matter what motivated him, she would remain impervious. She was committed to her course, and the most she would entertain was a momentary diversion.

In regard to her own motives, she wanted to be frank. She was attracted to his strength, his carved profile and the vulnerability she sensed in him that matched her own. She was attracted to the way his eyes crinkled when he smiled, and his laconic sense of humor. And she couldn't stop thinking about Molly's comment. She had no doubt the maid was right, and he knew his way around a woman's body. Knew how to bring her pleasure. More pleasure than she could find with her own hand beneath the worn sheets at night. Certainly more pleasure than the mechanical fucking she'd been subjected to at the behest of her deceased husband. He was the perfect candidate to explore her own desires and needs. The perfect tutor for seduction.

The snow was thickening around them and she was certain it meant she and her charges would be stranded at his manor. It was an ideal interlude and didn't interfere with her plans to secure her sisters' future happiness and security.

She braced her hands on her hips. "Why do you want me in your arms?"

"You're a generous handful. All those curves I want to glide my hands over. Sleep has been an implausible difficulty because I can't stop thinking about the way your body felt lying against mine in the straw. The way you stretched and bent against me while you slumbered. The soft, recumbent weight of your limbs against mine. The way you sighed, like the brush of a gentle breeze in the sails, when you adjusted your position."

"As you know, I'm in no position to entertain a dalliance. My situation is precarious and subject to the whims of my stepson. When I tell you I am completely at his mercy, I'm not exaggerating." What she refused to share was the promise Hugh had made to see her sisters secure. She couldn't indulge her own weakness at the risk of imperiling that offer. Her sisters deserved a fate better than her own. They deserved to steer the helm in the direction of their own choices. Arie knew that their protests to the opposite effect were made of naivete. She'd learned firsthand how merciless circumstances could be, and she didn't intend to allow any of them to be reduced to that. She wanted them to have the choices and the resources she didn't have.

"I can be discreet, madam."

"So you are propositioning me. Is this your way of showing me how ungentlemanly you can be?"

He shrugged and grinned.

He was very hard to resist.

"I can be discreet as well. But the truth has a way of coming out. Whatever discretion you believe you have the power to exercise needs to be magnified tenfold." She couldn't afford to let her wayward desires impede her sisters' chances.

"If you're granting me permission to be ungentlemanly, I'm resolved to do exactly that," he lifted her gloved hand to his mouth, pushed aside the frayed edge, and brushed his lips over the sensitive skin of her wrist. "Shall we proceed to Simon House?"

His touch discomfited her, and she turned away to escape his knowing scrutiny.

The shrieking and giggling of Ruby and Pearl as they clamored to be set upon the gray gelding provided the perfect opportunity to ignore him. The sturdy horse had remained resolute in the traces when his fellow pacer spooked and caused them to careen off the road. She turned to watch them and couldn't help shaking her head at the smiles that wreathed their faces and the rosy cast of their cherubic cheeks. With the typical resilience and insouciance of youth, the girls had embraced the adventure of the rescue and the prospect of playmates. The perilous nature of what could've happened to them had been glossed over. She wished she had that luxury. The luxury to trust things would work out for the better no matter what.

Arie was so preoccupied by her musings and trying to devise a plausible explanation for proceeding with the journey instead of turning back, the feel of his grip on her waist sent a jolt of tingling awareness down her spine.

"What are you doing?"

"We don't have a mounting block, and while I don't doubt your ability to clamber onto Roland's back on your own, this way is much easier," he explained as he hoisted her over his mount. Arie scrambled to an upright position, her skirts rucked above her knees, her scarlet wool stockings bared. She tangled her hands in the rough silk of the horse's mane, and almost missed the gleam of the possessive glance he leveled toward her legs like a shot across the bow of a ship.

Flustered once again, she returned her gaze to Ruby and Pearl. Arie was determined to quell the effect that loaded glance had on her insides. Despite her resolution to remain unaffected, she caught her breath when he swung up behind her and held herself rigidly away from the carved wall of his chest. She feared she'd lose all sense of decorum and end up sprawled in his lap if she relented. It was the thought of those thighs and the way they'd flexed and rippled as he strained to lift the carriage. They were snugged around her waist, muscled and mouthwatering and warmly sheltering her own.

"Nay," he murmured. He pulled her back, until she was flush against him, looping his arms around her in an inescapable embrace. "As I've already confessed, I've been dreaming of the way you felt in my arms, and I'll not allow you to retreat and deny either of us the pleasure. I'm not about to forfeit this chance to verify the truth of my memories," he rumbled into the shell of her ear. It was the same rumble he'd teased her with when they parted the first time. She wanted to scratch away at the spot – all too aware of the rasp of his bristled cheek. "And the ground may be rough. I don't want you tumbling onto it because you're unseated."

He wasn't going to allow her to keep a remote distance between them, so she obliged him. Even though every single thing about this journey through the snow would be indelibly imprinted on her body. She reclined against the comfort he offered and lost herself to the light salt scent of his sweat, the leather and jangle of the saddle, and the musky, indescribable smell of the horse finding its stride beneath them. He lifted a gloved hand and adjusted her scarf, so it cascaded in folds over her ears and covered her nose. The tenderness of the gesture nearly undid her, and she was achingly grateful he couldn't see the sheen of tears suddenly burning her eyes.

The storm was intensifying. Its ferocity swirled around them, the road a dark ribbon ahead of them winding nowhere. The only certainty was the sturdy brace of his arms around her, the feel of iron thighs cradling her own, and the visible puffs of their mingled breath. The shift of the horse beneath them and the cage of his forearms created a cocoon against the world.

The rocking motion and the warmth lulled her to sleep. "We're here," the rumble of his baritone nudged her outside of the lull she'd succumbed to.

She forced her eyes open, and even with her lids at half-mast and the swirl and bite of the snow around them, she could make out the cozy manor that lay directly ahead. It was a jumble of Tudor architecture, with two wings flanking the main entry. She could easily imagine the leap and laughter of children chasing each other through its halls and felt a pang of sympathy for all the man sitting stalwartly behind her had lost.

The scarf fluttered around her neck, and she clasped the ends with one hand to keep the invasion of the intensifying cold at bay. Thaddeus swung himself to the ground and reached for her. The close dismount meant she slid against the hardness of his body. Arie felt every hard plane against her curves and glanced away, suddenly shy. She was afraid to meet his gaze because of the unspoken promise spooling between them. She was afraid of the temptation she would recklessly embrace if she did.

***

Thaddeus had been reluctant to relinquish her and let the world intrude. He'd been checking fences on the southern edge of his property and their coachman had come upon him completely by chance. Snowflakes had already been swirling about and he shuddered to think what would've happened if he hadn't been there to help extract his visitors from their carriage and ensure they arrived safely at their destination.

In the daylight, she was even more delectable. He could easily get lost in her dark eyes with swirls of gray like those of dove feathers, the rich gleam of her deep chestnut hair gilded with russet highlights and the occasional metallic streak. Her face was determined and piquant, with rounded cheeks and a delicately pointed chin that he wanted to bite when she belligerently angled it toward him. Her figure, even swathed in layers, was sheer temptation. His thoughts careened back to his restless dreams of unwrapping her.

She turned away to go to Ruby and Pearl and his light grip on her wrist slid until their fingers were tangled together. He tugged her forward until they were both watching the coachman carefully lift the girls from their mount. They ran to her, cheeks flushed. "Please Arie, please convince father we are ready to graduate from our ponies," pleaded Pearl.

"I shall make a case for you, but must caution you against getting your hopes up, darlings. Your father may not see the sense in populating the stables with horses that won't be used for the hunt or other purposes."

Thad wasn't surprised. The envious schoolboy Hugh Greaves once was, and hadn't outgrown, would eschew the indulgence of frivolity in everyone but his wife or himself.

"I'm sure I can make my stables available if the girls wish to ride more substantial mounts than their ponies," he offered.

Arie cast him a grateful glance beneath her lids, and he held his breath, waiting for her answer. If she chose to accept the offer on behalf of Hugh's daughters, it would be up to her to make sure it happened. To make the appropriate explanations or decide to hide the purpose of the visits. It would be up to her to accompany them.

"I think that could be arranged," she softly agreed.

Thaddeus let go of the breath he'd been holding, relieved beyond measure, and clasped her hand again. He placed it in the crook of his elbow as they strode toward the imposing oak doors. The warmth when they crossed the foyer provided instant relief.

She began to unwind the scarf, but it somehow tangled in the low chignon at her nape. He stepped forward to assist, confident she wouldn't refuse his help. His hands settled on her shoulders, and he felt the shiver course across them as he slowly extricated her from her awkward position. When she turned around he was smiling down at her. "My thanks for your timely rescue," she stammered.

Thaddeus was eminently pleased his touch made her tongue-tied. He didn't know whether she was speaking of the escape from winter's wrath or the unwieldy scarf, but he relished her discomfort. "The pleasure was mine," he assured her. "Welcome to our humble abode. I am beyond grateful you made it in one piece, and that I could be of service ensuring your safety."

Her cheeks flushed and she slid her gaze away. And was promptly, enthusiastically greeted by the sight of four impatient, dark-haired imps quivering with barely concealed excitement. Much like the mound of wriggling puppies they'd been surrounded by at their first meeting. He could tell his daughters wanted to jump up and down in their excitement. He shook his head. "How have you miscreant children occupied yourselves today?" he asked as he squatted to catch them in a hug.

"Papa, Nan let us help her make bread!" Callie informed him with a squeal.

"And she said that Mama's first batch was burnt up a lot worse than ours," Rissa smugly explained.

"They insisted, and you know Grandmother is intent on teaching us to manage a household." Clem informed him.

"They wouldn't let me help," pouted his youngest, Claire, as she flailed against his shoulder.

His companion's tinkling laughter surrounded them, and the girls turned their attention to her. She lowered herself to the ground, so she was on eye-level with the youngest, and they rushed toward her. They halted their headlong dash mere inches away, as if they'd belatedly remembered an admonishment that young ladies should behave with decorum and grace. "Papa has told us so much about you."

He wanted to groan. Who knew how she would interpret that piece of damning information?

She raised her gaze to his, one brow quirked in surprise. He could tell from the speculative glint she was wondering what exactly he'd told them based upon their very brief introduction. "I am happy to make your acquaintance as well," she clasped their hands. "You may call me Arie. My charges Ruby and Pearl have brought their favorite dolls and are hoping you will have tea with them."

"I'm Clarissa and she's Callista. Papa calls us Rissa and Callie. Our eldest sister is Clementine and the youngest is Claire. And we want to hear about the puppies and how you're going to train them to herd the sheep." The twin with curly hair piped up.

"And tea sounds lovely," gushed Callie, her eyes shining, and her hands clasped tightly around the squirming black cat she was carrying. She had it half slung over her shoulder, and it appeared to be wearing some sort of headpiece.

"It will be quite a while before they're old enough to begin their training. But I'll see if we can arrange a way for you to watch it. And perhaps even bring one of them home to tend your herds here." Arie reassured her.

Ruby stepped forward and thrust out her hand toward the younger girls. "I'm Ruby and I'm thirteen. I have tea parties with my sisters because even though I've grown too old for such things I know it makes them happy. I'll be a guest of yours as well."

The younger girls looked up at Ruby with worshipful, rapt expressions. Arie wanted to laugh, because she knew her eldest charge was fond of adoring minions that obeyed her every whim. "It seems Ruby has acquired more subjects," she wryly observed.

"My daughters are starved for outside female companionship, and Ruby likely seems like an exotic fairy princess." Thad replied.

When Ruby halted in front of Clementine, they regarded each other with wary expressions. As if they were sizing each other up for a bout in the ring. Clem was the first to capitulate. She held out her hand. "We can mind them together, wear them out, and then talk about the things we really want to talk about."

Ruby took Clem's hand and pumped it up and down in solidarity. "Yes, like handsome stableboys and hats."

"I fear Ruby may turn Clementine's head to more frivolous things," Arie observed.

"So long as they're just flights of fancy and not encouragement to go spying on the blacksmith's apprentices when they're bathing in the water trough, I have no qualms."

"She already has the stableboy that accompanied us, Jem, wrapped around her little finger. He's the one that smuggled the barn cats into the house that ruined the party."

Thad shrugged. "As much as I want to keep them from growing up, it's out of my hands. Clem is still enamored with dolls, so maybe Ruby's raptures over boys will fall on deaf ears."

"You do know that eventually your girls will have to grow up and entertain suitors?"

He groaned. "I do not look forward to that day. Stolen kisses were how Rachel and I ended up hitched long before we should have. Our eldest was nineteen and courting himself when he died."

"So you'll be one of those fathers that stands in a corner with a pitchfork and a shovel when the boys come calling." She chortled.

"I'll try not to be so obvious, although being protective of their hearts and their virtue can't be held against me. I'll need a helpmeet to navigate those treacherous waters."

He twined his fingers around her elbow where it winged toward him, wrapping his hand around the sinew of her arm. "Shall we?" He asked.

He hoped she felt the proprietary touch like a brand underneath the fabric she'd used to shore up the raveling serge of her gown.

She nodded her acquiescence.

He hoped she knew resistance would be futile. Because just like the cat squirming in his daughter's arms, and the one that had ruined the holiday fete, he wanted to peer into all her cupboards and investigate all her nooks and crannies. He'd become nothing more than a creature of curiosity compelled by a fascination he refused to examine too closely.

"Yes," she cleared her throat, resuming the conversation. "The girls have chattered about nothing else for three days straight. They have been over the moon at the prospect of playmates. Ruby admitted she didn't mind the age gap because she needed a change of scenery and it would be like acquiring more little sisters."

He smiled. "As have the twins and Claire. Clem hasn't been as vocal because I think she feared her place would be usurped. There aren't many children of an age with them that live close enough for such an event."

"Just smelly boys who like chasing frogs and getting mud on our frocks," Rissa observed over her shoulder. "Betty likes chasing them away with her broom."

When she turned her gaze to his, he knew she was asking who exactly Betty was to the household. He dipped close to answer. "Betty is the wife of the village blacksmith. She helps out when my mother is unable to get away from my father's practice. In return, I help Sam in the forge whenever I have time to spare."

His time in the forge explained the muscles she couldn't stop staring at, and the way he towered over the other men in the parish like he was blocking out the sun. "You don't pay Betty for her time?" Her brows narrowed, like she was preparing to give him a very sharp set-down. Like she hoped he wasn't stingy with coins like her stepson and his wife.

He shook his head in bemused affection. "She wouldn't take it. She'd be insulted. I grew up carousing about the countryside with her sons and vowed to watch over them when we went to war together. I made sure they were in my regiment and did everything in my power to ensure they came out of it alive."

"Did they?" She must've heard something in his voice, the buried pain he always tried to swallow when he spoke of them.

He looked down at her appraisingly. "You're not one for the easy questions, are you Arie?"

The sound of her nickname on his lips sent a bright curl of want threading through her lower belly. When she didn't answer, just looked at him expectantly, he continued. "Nay, they didn't. I couldn't keep my best friend from dying of a bayonet wound courtesy of one of our melees. His younger brothers came home, battered but whole."

"And you blame yourself for his death," Arie quietly observed.

"Aye. I persuaded him to sign onto the 5th Dragoons with me. We were both eager for the connections we'd gain and to see more of the world than the roles we were confined to here. He didn't want to be the next village blacksmith. He was going to throw his lot in with me and help me build my farmstock. Instead he met the point of a Turkish bayonet on a muddy, cursed field in the other side of the world," his voice softened, rusty with sorrow. "I couldn't even give him a proper burial. His wife and sons are my responsibility."

She gripped his arm tighter, willing him to continue. She knew from experience that the more often you allowed your self-recriminations to have a voice, the less time they spent haunting you. "I am certain his mother and his wife do not blame you for his death."

"They both insist he followed me of his own accord. I still wish like hell I could've given him a proper burial. I didn't even have the chance to bring home his medals."

"You saved his brothers from a similar fate, I'm sure he's looking on somewhere with gratitude."

"His mother has reassured me of the very same thing on multiple occasions. But that doesn't negate the guilt at my failure to provide a physical place for her to grieve."

"It isn't your responsibility. It's the fault of other men's greed and their need to impress their will on others. It's the fault of those who indulge in ideals that put others at risk."

"A man enlists because he hears stories of glory, grandeur, and bravery. We had no idea we'd spend weeks lying on the cold, muddy ground dodging enemy sniper fire and scuttling behind trees."

"Although the bravery of our forces has been extolled throughout every corner of the empire, it doesn't sound like an easy conquest."

"'Twas doomed from the very beginning. We were plagued by the ineptitude of our commanders. Men who were unaccustomed to ambush, skirmishes and being grossly outnumbered."

"It sounds horrific."

He sighed deeply. "I'm still plagued by nightmares on occasion. I don't believe I'll ever banish them completely."

Arie wondered if his nightmares were the reason he seemed in no hurry to wed again. Did he fear a wife would grow weary of his night sweats? Did he fear a wife would lack the patience to forgive his avoidance of social events or wouldn't understand his need to find solitude when the grisly memories became too much to bear?

"Is that why you haven't sought to remarry?"

He broke their eye contact and bowed his head, burrowing his other hand deep into his pocket. "That's not all of it," he raised his head and looked her in the eyes again. "I tell myself it's because I'm trying to expand the farm. I have some capital set aside for a new land acquisition, but the potential seller isn't being cooperative."

"Which parcel would you like to add to your holdings?"

"Johnston owns forty acres that border one of my lower grazing fields. I'd like to add it, but he's being recalcitrant."

Her eyes narrowed in thought. "If you acquired forty additional hectares, your holdings would rival those of my stepson. I'd hazard a guess he's not too keen on that idea. He and Johnston are friends and I'm sure Hugh is dangling something over his head."

Thad nodded in agreement. "He is. I cornered Johnston at the party, and he admitted as much."

Arie scrunched her nose in distaste. "He's despicable. I can't say I'm surprised. What will you do? Do you need the extra grazing land?"

He barked a laugh. "You know how rocky this side of the county is. I'll take any spot of meadow I can lay my hands on. There are other parcels I could seek out, but they aren't adjacent, and it would be harder to move the herds around. I spend most of my energy doing that already because I want to provide for my daughters. What little bit of energy I have left at the end of the day goes to them. They insist I need to find them a mother, but I'm not so sure that's what I want. At least I haven't been."

What was he confessing? That her fears were realized and he was looking for a convenient stand-in? "I'm not sure I understand," she pulled him to a stop. "Is it that you fear a wife would be a hindrance, and just one more thing you have to take care of? One more person to drain your limited resources and distract you from the things you need to accomplish? And why have you changed your mind?" She rubbed her thumb over his knuckles.

"I'm almost persuaded a spouse would be anything but a hindrance and the right person could help alleviate my burdens. I'd hoped you were offering." He informed her with a wistful expression.

"You know I am not. You need someone with more resources at their disposal to ensure the girls make advantageous matches when the time is right. You need a bride who comes to you with either an intact dowry or no other obligations so the farm will see success that much sooner. And I fulfill neither of those requirements."

"You're the only woman I've met I would willingly choose. You're beautiful, witty, and courageous. You're not full of your own consequence but instead seek to improve the lives of everyone around you. Those are not qualities to be taken for granted."

"I genuinely appreciate your compliments, and I sense they are heartfelt. But I am not the woman you should choose if you want to make your farm a success. I have no standing in the community.

According to most of the gentry, I'll never be anything more than a trumped-up village girl who was strange enough to train dogs."

He shook his head at her assessment. "I think you underestimate your consequence. You have a reputation for fair and honest dealing with the village merchants, and the staff at Greaves Manor have nothing but praise for the way you manage the household. You would be an asset no matter where you landed. We do well enough here, and I think you'd only add to the reputation of my farm, not detract from it. If you consented to a true proposal, I think we'd find joy for the remainder of our days. And mind you, the girls have been exerting an obscene level of pressure on me to acquire a spouse. I was reluctant until our encounter in the stables."

"I'd be sorely tempted to accept a true proposal, but I cannot in good conscience encourage you. My stepson assured me there was no provision for me in the will. Not even a widow's portion. You and your daughters deserve an alliance with resources. And besides, I'm looking for an entirely different sort of affiliation," Arie clarified.

Thaddeus cleared his throat. "An entirely different sort of affiliation? I'm intrigued by your mysterious proposal. But I want to hear more about it when you're not standing in my foyer with your hands and cheeks red from cold, your skirts bedraggled and wrinkled, and your stomach growling for sustenance. I would be chastised as a horrid host before the village assembly."

She shrugged. "A chastisement is unlikely. I'd be surprised beyond belief if anyone realized I was gone. It's common for the girls to eat in the nursery, and the revelry won't end for another five days at least. It'll likely last longer if the snow makes the roads impassable."

"I'd wager the fox hunt scheduled for tomorrow will be cancelled. All the foxes are likely snuggled up in their burrows – as we all should be. There's a copper slipper bath in the bedroom located in the left wing. I'll stoke a fire for you and then leave the hot water outside your door. I put indoor plumbing in the kitchen last year, but I've yet to put in a bathing room."

"I can start my own fire if there's a coal bucket. But I would immensely appreciate a warm bath- and some rosemary water if you have it so I can brush out my hair and wash it."

"And you claim you have no resources. As I've said before, you are accustomed to taking care of yourself and everyone around you. So accustomed I doubt they even notice how much more comfortable you make their lives," his hand curved around her jaw. "I'll conjure some rosemary and soap from the cook and let you bathe in privacy. I've given you the suite on the top floor of the west wing, so you'll be somewhat secluded and left to your own devices. I can't imagine you get much of that in your current station."

"I do not, and I sincerely appreciate it. I can't remember the last time I was able to indulge in an uninterrupted, luxurious bath."

"Unfortunately, I can't provide perfumed soap. But the honey blend Betty makes and is kind enough to share is particularly soothing, and I'll bring some up with the water," he paused, pinning her hand to his arm. "And after you feel refreshed, perhaps you can tell me more about your audacious proposal."

May You Bloom and Grow

The girls decided it was time to bombard him when he went to tuck them in.

"Father, Ruby wants to do know why you kissed Arie on the forehead. And so do we," Rissa demanded.

"I kissed her on the forehead because I was relieved," he explained.

"You didn't kiss us on our foreheads," Pearl mutinously pointed out.

"Well I'd yet to make the acquaintance of you and your sister. I knew Arie when she was a girl and we were recently reintroduced."

"You knew Arie when she was a little girl like us?" Claire asked. Her eyes were saucers of astonishment.

"Yes, she wasn't much older than Clem, and she and her sisters used to play in the village square. Your grandfather attended her family when her mother was dying."

"That must have been sad," Clem mournfully intoned.

"It was. And Arie became a mother to her younger sisters."

"She wasn't allowed to be a little girl anymore?" They all cried out in unison, as if they'd been practicing, their expressions horrified.

"She was not. Not in the way you're allowed to be. She had to think of others first and always. She's been doing it her whole life, I'd wager."

Ruby nodded in agreement. "She only has three dresses and Mother laughs and says they all look like they came from the ragpicker's bin."

The spiteful nature of Greaves' wife made him cringe and want to box her ears. "Mayhap she doesn't have anyone willing to buy her new dresses."

Pearl's brow furrowed in concentration. "But we always get new dresses when we ask for them."

"You are the daughters of the squire and it's his duty to make sure you are well provided for and are a suitable reflection of his station. Arie isn't related to the squire."

"But she used to be his stepmama," Pearl insisted.

A fact Thad was certain Hugh repudiated to the depths of his curmudgeonly soul. "She was also your grandfather's wife. But she no longer has that status. I'm sure she does the best she can with what she has. You should be more understanding of her paltry wardrobe."

"We would never say anything to hurt her feelings or make her sad," Ruby assured him.

If even her charges noticed the derelict state of her wardrobe, it must be truly pathetic. He would do what he could to remedy its lack while she was here. He'd force her to accept his charity. He suspected the snow was only just beginning and would blanket and isolate them by morning.

"You should always treat her with respect. Her life has already had too much sadness."

"We love Arie," Pearl piped up. "We should tell her more. She's always right beside me when I fall and skin my knee. And she's teaching us to fish and climb trees."

Thad laughed. "Both admirable pursuits for little girls."

Rissa turned to Pearl and Ruby with an eager expression she didn't bother disguising. "If she's already teaching you, do you think she'd teach us those things too?"

"I'm sure she would," Ruby confirmed. "She told us girls had the right to learn those things as much as boys, and it would make us more self-sufficient," she proudly concluded.

All four of his daughters turned to him next. "Can we ask her to teach us, Papa?"

He reached over and chucked every single chin. "Of course you can. It's not likely your Gran knows how to do those things."

"Or if she did, she probably forgot how to do them because she's so old. She told us yesterday her knees felt like they were as old as the hills, and we shouldn't run away when she was trying to make us behave." Complained Callie.

"You shouldn't run from your grandmother," he chastised.

"Not even if she wants us to sit all day and learn how to hem shirts and knead bread?" Rissa petulantly asked.

"Not even then. Those are things you need to learn. Learning them is even more important than learning how to climb trees and catch a fish."

"Why are they so important?"

Sometimes, especially times like this, Thad really wished he had a wife by his side who could diplomatically explain what would be expected of his daughters when they reached adulthood. He didn't agree with the strict adherence to gender roles practiced in the parish and supported the suffrage movement. But things would most assuredly go easier for Rissa and Callie if they mastered the skills his mother was intent on teaching them.

"You need to learn those things so you can take care of your own households someday."

"I won't need to know how to do those things." Rissa declared with a decisive nod of her head. Like she was making a resolution.

"And why is that pet?" he queried in amusement. His headstrong daughter had very clear ideas about what she wanted from life. Even at the age of eight and a half.

"Because I'm going to grow up to be a princess."

"You have to be born a princess, you don't grow up to be one," Clem scoffed.

"That's not true! What if I marry the prince?"

"And how will your prince find you in the wilds of Cumbria?" Thaddeus prodded, curious to hear her answer.

"He'll come here looking for me," Rissa replied with determination.

"Princes live in castles. There aren't any castles here." Observed her more pragmatic twin.

He smoothed the unruly curls from her sweaty temples. "I still think you should listen to your grandmother."

"Just because I listen to her doesn't mean I'm not going to be a princess."

"No, it just means you'll be able to take better care of the prince when you meet him."

"Okay, Papa. We promise not to run away from Grandmother when we're bored," Rissa penitently vowed.

"That's all I can ask. Now, I want all of you to go to sleep instead of staying up half the night chattering. Ruby and Clem are the eldest, so you should listen to them and let them know if you need anything."

"Papa, do you think there will be a lot of snow when we wake up in the morning?" Clem's eyes were shiny with excitement.

"Yes, poppet. I think we're going to be snowed in for quite a while. That means Arie, Ruby and Pearl will be our guests and you must be on your best behavior."

"Will they still be here for Christmas? It's only three days away!" Callie shouted.

"Yes, we'll most likely be in each other's company for Christmas."

"That means we have a lot of planning."

Any time Rissa mentioned plans, he'd learned to expect the unexpected. He gave her a stern glance, even though he knew dissuading her was a fool's endeavor. "You need to keep the shenanigans at a minimum, Rissa."

"I just meant we'll need to make sure everyone has presents, that's all."

He didn't believe her, but he wasn't going to press the issue right now. "I hope that's all you meant. Now, it's been a long day and we all need to find our rest."

Even though he'd been outside in the brisk wind all day, and his muscles ached from setting fenceposts and removing the carriage from the mud, he was looking forward to seeing his other houseguest.

I Have Confidence the World Can All Be Mine

The kind of arrangement Arie was considering was prescribed to time and place. The blizzard presented the perfect opportunity to explore the sensual side of her nature she'd never embraced. Despite his confession he was attracted to her, she sensed her host was reluctant to indulge his inclinations. She decided to channel the scandalous diaries of Isabella Robinson and present her rescuer with a tableau he'd find impossible to resist. As soon as she divested herself of her undergarments, she yanked the sheet off the bed and wrapped it around her body. She reclined indolently in the chair before the fire. Stretching her toes toward it and awaiting his return.

She was going to take advantage of the opportunity to find out exactly why adventurous widows sought out lovers, and why women who figured so prominently in London's gossip columns pursued dreams outside the marriage bed.

As he'd promised, he lightly rapped his knuckles against the door, and the soft thunk of the water pails on the wood floors echoed down the hallway. "Please bring them in," she called out. "I find myself exhausted by our ordeal this afternoon."

"You're sure?" he asked solicitously. "I don't want to disturb you."

"I am very sure."

"Your wish is my command. If you'll open the door, I'll bring them in."

She decided the sheet wasn't actually necessary. The only purpose it served was hindering her plans for seduction. She wanted to destroy any illusions he harbored regarding her reticence or modesty.

She dropped the sheet to the floor and swung open the door, casually leaning against it with her hand planted on her hip.

"I see you wasted no time preparing the fire or getting ready for your bath." She heard the sudden hitch in his breathing as his eyes scanned her from head to toe. She shivered as she imagined that burning gaze was the skimming caress of his hands. She was very thankful he'd given her a room where they were less likely to be interrupted or disturbed.

He brushed past her, and she shut the door with a solid thud. Then she latched it. Nothing could've made her intentions clearer. "Would you like to talk about the type of alliance I'm proposing?"

"I may have trouble concentrating," he admitted as he averted his eyes. "I think your absence of clothing is a reliable indication of your intentions. You won't need to explain much." He was gripping the bucket handles with white knuckles, his forearms corded from the strain of holding them.

"I can help with that. Why don't you place the buckets by the hearth and have a seat?"

He carefully set them on the floor and warily settled into the wing-back chair.

She twined the sheet around her body again and approached him. "I've never experienced the raptures I've heard the maids incessantly talk about and swoon over. I believe you're in a unique position to show me what all the fuss is truly about. I have it on good authority you can show me what I've been missing."

A rush of crimson saturated his cheekbones. She'd embarrassed him. "How am I to show you?" he rasped.

"You can give me a carnal demonstration," she elaborated.

His cheeks became a deeper crimson, and his brows were like slashes of thunder as his gaze skated over her again. "A carnal demonstration? Why am I uniquely qualified for such a demonstration? What good authority gave you this information?"

"All the maids talk about you. Apparently you had quite the reputation before you were wed. And you told me you had quite the brood. Which means you should know what you're about. And you basically propositioned me after our encounter in the barn when you offered to show me just how ungentlemanly you can be if I encourage your behavior."

His brow arched nearly to his hairline. "How do you know the offer wasn't just part of our light-hearted flirting? What makes you think it was made in earnest?"

"Flirting is just a way to disguise what you really want with a veneer of social niceties. Usually it's a thinly veiled indication that you want to fuck the object of your admiration. I don't think you were just flirting. You wouldn't be so nervous right now."

He grinned and leaned back in the chair, surveying her with a hooded gaze. "Such forthright language, Widow Greaves. But it's a fair assessment. Although perhaps not all flirting should be so swiftly indicted. On occasion it is merely a way to indulge in banal, harmless conversation with someone of the opposite sex. You have to admit that in-depth conversations are not encouraged on a ballroom floor."

She smiled. "I concede your point. Your powers of observation are further evidence of your attention to detail."

"And my attention to detail makes you confident of my prowess? A man's ability to spread his seed doesn't mean he knows how to please a woman. One has nothing to do with the other."

"I'm certain you don't lack company. Especially if the enthusiasm of the chambermaids is any indication of your popularity with the opposite sex. They sang nothing but praises when I asked them about you the morning after the stable. I'd wager you're in high demand."

"I was gone for four and a half years, and I've been very selective and circumspect in the three years since my return. I don't want an inconvenient or scandalous liaison to influence the way my daughters are treated by the rest of society and those in the village."

Yes, he'd been gone for nearly half of her marriage. And returned not long before she became single again. She wished she were brazen enough to ask him outright to be her lover for as long as they wished to form a connection. She wished her heart didn't quake in the soles of her feet at the thought of the censure she'd endure from the village if such an arrangement became public knowledge. Unfortunately, he was right. The strictures of a country parish were far harsher than the approbations of the peerage. If he openly flaunted an illicit relationship, his daughters would be snubbed by their peers. Her situation was similar. If she publicly took a lover her stepson would suffer no compunction casting her out into the muddy street with nothing. He'd probably make her go shoeless. He'd lead the charge to brand her with a scarlet letter like the heroine of the Hawthorn novel she'd just read.

But that didn't mean she couldn't seize this golden opportunity. No one but the two of them was here to witness her fall from grace and she intended to take full advantage of the lack of prying eyes. She could ogle those thighs and feel his scruff against her skin. She could ask him to hold her after she was done climbing him like a tree.

"If you were faithful to your wife during your time away, you're a singular man," she remarked. Most of the men she knew didn't think fidelity was a requirement of marriage.

"I was faithful. But Rachel and I enjoyed energetic bed sport and had known each other since childhood. We were sweethearts most of our lives. Mayhap I didn't want to settle for anything less than that sort of commitment. Mayhap that's why I've avoided entanglements since my return from Crimea."

"You do realize you just authenticated my choice? I find it extremely hard to believe that you'd decline such an indulgence when it clearly benefits the both of us."

He groaned and her heart stopped. "You make it extremely hard to resist you, Araminta Greaves."

"I want you to find me irresistible, Thaddeus St. Simon," she teased and loosened her hold on the sheet, so it slowly slid to the floor.

"Come here," he beckoned as his eyes roved over every part of her exposed to his view.

She sauntered toward him, girded in false bravado. By the time she reached his chair, the bravado was no longer completely manufactured. He looked at her like she was a plateful of blackberry jam roly poly and cream, or bread pudding. He reached out, trailing his hand down her cleavage and circling her hip. He tugged until she fell against him.

"Straddle me, Arie," he commanded, his voice edged in gravel.

The steel in his order made her fingertips tingle. She was eager to obey and lowered herself over his lap. He leaned forward, his hand cupped to cradle her face. She met his touch, bending toward him until the curve of her cheek and chin were nestled against his rough warmth. And then he was smoothing back loose tendrils of hair, combing his fingers through her disheveled curls.

She was thirty-eight and she'd never been truly kissed. She'd enjoyed a surreptitious, sloppy embrace or two courtesy of her boyhood suitors at the village fair. That was the sum of her experience. To her husband she'd been a perfunctory obligation. Lying on her stomach so he could ogle her "luscious bum". Clothes on, her dress flung to her waist, a few grunts and that was it. No thought of bringing her pleasure. She wouldn't have known such a thing even existed if she hadn't overheard the chambermaids discussing their amorous adventures and found the secret stash of naughty diaries and memoirs in her husband's library. They'd provided quite the education. She wanted to try all of those things. And this might be her only chance. He might be her only chance.

She saw something indescribable in his eyes. Something she never thought she'd see in a man's eyes when he looked at her. A tender regard that made her heart stutter in her chest. A smoldering gaze that both cherished and devoured.

She wanted that first true kiss and she wanted him to be the one who bestowed it. This emotionally scarred, teasing soldier who wore his heart on his sleeve. The way he was with his daughters, indulgent yet stern. The way he'd been in the stable, giving her a safe, warm place to rest and then poking gentle fun at her afterwards. She edged forward, her knees bracketing his. She let the tip of her tongue lap at his capable palm. A palm that settled precious cargo onto the backs of cantankerous ponies. A palm that soothed playful puppies and delivered piglets, lambs, and calves. A palm that had lifted both children and rifles to his shoulder. A palm she wanted to feel smoothed against every inch of her skin.

He groaned, a deep baritone, and closed his eyes. "I should not want to touch you as much as I do. I should not dream of you like this, with your rosy, satin soft lips full of temptation, and those luscious curves that are driving me mad. You're like the first hint of dawn creeping over the hills. Full of promise. Inimitable. Irresistible. You're more than I ever dreamed would be sitting here, a beautiful, bountiful blessing in my lap, beneath my hands. You make me want things I shouldn't, Arie."

"I'm neither inimitable nor irresistible. Otherwise I wouldn't be asking for a demonstration of your amorous skills. And you should tell me about the things you think you shouldn't want."

"You may regret asking me once you hear them," his gaze intensified and his thumb over the curve of her cheek. "I want to tie you to that bed and shove a chair under the door and keep you here for days. I want to sit in that tub with you and run the sponge over your breasts and your sweet little cunny. I want to dip my fingers and my tongue inside you and taste your release. I want to bring you ecstasy, but I won't compromise your reputation by indulging in more or encouraging a lengthier liaison."

His fierce confession unmoored her. "We're isolated here. Most of the parish is either hibernating because of the storm or ensconced in luxury at the manor I departed this morning. What they won't know won't hurt them. Why shouldn't we indulge while we can? Why shouldn't we enjoy each other when it's just us in this room and no one to gainsay our desires?"

"We aren't completely isolated. My daughters and your charges are uncannily observant and are bound to notice any hint of an attachment. And you know the servants will talk. I'm sure your coachman isn't averse to tipping the occasional pint at the pub. And neither is my groom. If we're reckless, we'll be found out."

"I'm a ready and willing student of whatever lesson you wish to give. Even a glimpse of the things I've missed is better than never experiencing them at all."

"Who am I to dissuade you?" He murmured.

He stretched out his legs, pressing her against the hard planes of his body. His shirt was dampened by sweat, unbuttoned nearly to his waist, barely hanging from one shoulder. She slid her hands inside, suddenly desperate to spread them across that tantalizing expanse of bare skin. There was a light sheen of sweat between his pectoral muscles, and she leaned forward to taste its tang against her tongue. She trailed her hand down the whorling path of hair that spread across the slabs of muscle and narrowed as it angled downward, greedily chasing it to the point it disappeared in his breeches.

She remembered how the muscles in his back and buttocks clenched when he lifted the carriage wheel from the mud and moaned aloud. She stretched against the hard ridge of his arousal and a toe-curling delicious rumble emerged from his chest.

"You're like lightning in my veins." She confessed as she curled her fingers into the crisp sweep of dark hair feathering across his chest again, using it as an anchor. She urged him closer, until their breaths mingled. It sounded harsh in the quiet of the room, a punctuated staccato to the sizzle and crackle of the fire in front of them. "I've never wanted to explore anything so much as I want to explore your body and allow you to explore mine."

He closed his eyes and took a deep breath at her admission. It was obvious he was struggling to hold onto the reins of composure. "I can and will stop at any time. You need only say the word. So long as I can touch you, I will sit in this very place with your enticing warmth and scent draped around me."

"Please touch me." Her brain was so scrambled with anticipation, she barely managed to get the words out of her mouth. She was quivering with the tautness of a bowstring.

He dropped his lips to hers and slid his hands up her torso. He palmed the weight of her breasts in his hands. She sighed into the kiss, opening her mouth to him. The kiss was like sinking and falling and being found and being lost. It infused her with sweetness, making her crave it and miss it even though she was still in the middle of it. His tongue stroked her bottom lip, and then dove in to tangle with her own. "I want you to touch me as well," he groaned into the kiss.

Arie slid her hand between them, nimbly unbuttoning his pants and spreading apart the placket. Even though she'd never done anything so brazen, she wasn't going to allow her lack of experience to deter her. When she closed her hands around his cock he surged against her. She rose to her knees so she could get a firmer grip. He relinquished the kiss, letting his head rest against the back of the chair. "Is this how you want me to touch you?" she asked. She didn't recognize herself. She felt like a woman in full possession of her sexual power.

"I should be the one touching you. I thought that was the deal we made."

"The deal we struck was for my enlightenment. Stroking your cock is just as enlightening as the way your fingers will feel hooked inside me."

"I don't feel enlightened. I feel unhinged," he growled.

She tapped a finger against his chin. "My enlightenment, not yours. Remember?"

"Christ, how could I forget?" he sighed in surrender.

"If this is about what I want, there are things I've been fixated on doing to you that require an accessory."

"An accessory?" He sounded vaguely alarmed.

"Yes. An accessory. Or two. Stay just as you are," she hopped off his lap, searching the room. One of the drapery cords would serve her purposes. And she had a wide kerchief she tied around her hair when she was doing her laundry to keep the mist of harsh lye from affecting her curls. She'd stuffed it in the pocket of her cloak after she'd finished scrubbing her black bombazine in the outdoor trough. It would do as well.

She gathered them and brandished the items in the air. "Do you still trust me?"

"Yes. " he finished grimly as he eyed the objects in her hands.

She halted behind his chair. "Hands, please."

He obliged, his gaze dark and hungry over his shoulder as she wound the cord around his wrists, making sure it was secure. "You're binding me?" She could hear disbelief and a thread of subdued excitement in his voice.

"Yes. And blindfolding you," she slipped her hands into his hair and removed the piece of twine that secured his queue. She let her hands slide through the silky ink and his breath sped up. She used the inky skeins to tug him closer. She folded the kerchief four times, so he wouldn't be able use his sense of sight, slipped it past his ears and tied it as securely as the cord around his wrists.

His breath sped up even more. "I can't see anything. Not even a shadow. I'm completely at your mercy. And you're very adventurous for a prim widow, Arie. Far more adventurous than I gave you credit for."

"Well, as you've clearly deduced, I'm far from the prim façade I present to the world. I've always been the powerless one, and I knew you'd let me upset the balance. I thought you might like being at my mercy. And this may be the only chance to see just how uninhibited

I can be." She felt like one of the wilderness surveyors she'd heard of in America, or one of the archaeologists who'd first glimpsed the Giza Valley. There was a veritable bounty spread before her. The thought of discovering and mapping it, of intentionally uncovering its treasures, made her giddy. A chest bisected by a trail the color of bituminous coal, with a few threads of white that matched the occasional streaks on his head. A jagged, angry scar arced over the left side of his ribcage, and his right shoulder and upper arm were pocked with divots. She leaned forward and grazed the divots with her mouth, "Are these from the war?" she murmured, wishing she could take away even the memory of the hurt.

"Yes, they're from shrapnel. The one along my side is from the slice of a Russian saber I couldn't duck away from in time."

The danger he'd been in, the stoic way he treated the trauma of his survival and the death of those close to him, made her want to beg him to lay his head in her lap in a field of wildflowers so she could stroke his hair away from his forehead, sing him a lullaby and urge him to cast aside all the worries that kept him from restorative sleep.

She shoved down the urge to comfort him. Not because he didn't need it. But because if she offered it she was letting him know she saw beneath all his carefully constructed layers. If she acted on her impulses, he'd immediately recognize the reflection of ignored pain and self-denial in her own eyes.

Instead of admitting her vulnerability or his own, she abandoned her exploration and reclaimed his lap. Her back was to his chest this time. She draped her legs on either side of his granite hewn thighs, loving the way the position stretched her hamstrings to the point of near pain. She undulated against the throbbing length of cock against the small of her back and he growled in response. "I want to see you claim your power, but the thought of you having your way with my body is driving me mad." He thrust his hips upward, gliding between the cleft of her buttocks. She let him guide the rhythm and slid her hands toward her breasts. She lightly pinched her nipples, imagining what it would feel like to have the sharp edge of his teeth graze over them or the delicate abrasion of his beard. The vision of that dark head bent over her in abject worship made her shudder.

"You're touching yourself, aren't you, vixen? Even though I can't see it because of this infernal mask, I can feel it in the sway of your body."

"Yes. And imagining it's your mouth instead," she taunted. "You've scooped up a handful of gooseberry jam and you're painting my breasts and my belly with those big, rough hands so you can lick it off."

He must have been enticed by the picture she painted, because he thrust against her even more erratically. It was an iron grind between her thighs that made her tug even more forcefully on her breasts, until her nipples were so sensitive the barest swipe of her thumb made her rear back against him.

"I'm going to empty every last drop of my cock against your back because you tied me up and I can't catch it with my hands," he thrust against her, and she felt the length of him stroke up her spine like a brand. "I'm going to paint your back with my cum and picture you laid out on the table where we take our meals, your cunt rosy and swollen from the scratch of my beard against your inner thighs, your legs around my neck as I break my fast with the taste of you in my mouth," he warned in a low rasp that made her skin tingle.

"Go ahead. Spend. I want to revel in your scent coating my body."

Her words were the catalyst and she felt him tense behind her. "Bloody hell, woman...your words...Fuck!" He roared. And he ejaculated against the curve of her spine as she bent forward and gripped his thighs.

She rose from his lap and turned around so she could see the aftermath of her manipulation. His cheekbones and the bridge of his nose were flushed, the waves of midnight hair streaked in white at the temples falling across his face in complete disarray. He was sprawled languidly in the chair, his spent cock lax against his stomach. It glistened under the gaslight, and she wanted to lick it clean. Suddenly, nothing mattered more than seeing the expression in his eyes. Her fingers slipped beneath the knot of the blindfold, loosening it so it fell to his throat. "I want to lick you clean," she confessed aloud.

"I wouldn't say no, vixen."

"Instead, I'm going to employ this." She pulled the handkerchief loose and wrapped it around him, soaking up the evidence of his inability to resist her. Once she was finished stroking him to half-mast again, she dropped the bunch of material to the floor.

Arie walked over to the ewer with an exaggerated sway and snagged the drying cloth from the side table. She dipped it into the water and arched her neck. The droplets cascaded down her body as she swiped his semen from her back.

His eyes were blazing, his lips parted, when she dropped the cloth and strolled toward him.

"You haven't found your release," he drowsily protested, surveying her from beneath hooded lids. "And that's what this temporary alliance is about. You want me to show you all the things you missed out on in the squire's bed."

"I have no doubts whatsoever you'll ensure I find my release," she reassured him. "But I love seeing you like this. Completely undone for want of me."

"I'm undone, but not done. You shouldn't patronize me," he warned. "Because every skill I've honed since I was an experimental youth over twenty years ago will be used against you."

She sighed in contentment. "I wasn't patronizing you. I knew the maids were right about your skill."

"And my considerable skill will make you forget your name, and your surrender will make me forget mine. Especially now we've taken the serrated edge off our desire. You can untie me now so we can finish what you've started. I'm not finished showing you how ungentlemanly I can be."

She walked behind him on shaky legs, her body hovering on the sharp edge of want. When she untied him, he sprang from the chair, and stalked toward her. The dark glint in his eyes made her stomach quiver anew, and she could see her reflection in his gaze. Wary prey flushed from its hiding place, mesmerized by the stealthy intent of the creature hunting it. She felt like a hare about to be devoured by a wolf. The urge to squeal and run shot through her, eager to make him give chase. But her muscles felt loose, and she briefly wondered if crawling would be easier than walking. Her entire body was caught in some paroxysm between desire and fear. So she stood immobile until he caught her up in his arms and threw her over his shoulder.

She gasped in mock outrage, secretly thrilled by his show of dominance. "I thought I was in control," she belatedly protested as he tossed her to the bed.

"You're still in control. I'm nothing more than your puppet right now, and you're pulling the strings. It's my responsibility to make sure you have *un petit mort* that will make the angels weep." He crawled up the length of her body, braced himself on his forearms, and dropped his forehead to hers.

"I want to whisper all the ways I want to ravage you into the adorable shell of your ear. I want to stroke your pretty clit with my thumb, so you need to grab the headboard," he coaxed as he leveled himself out with one arm and clamped his other hand to her hip. He slid it across her navel and dropped it, so she could feel the heat like a brand over the part of her still tingling and throbbing from their foreplay on the chair.

She wanted to slither away in a pool of want. The maids hadn't been exaggerating.

He tapped her clitoris with the steady rhythm of a marching cadence. The pulse he created skittered through her veins and she wrapped her legs around his lean hips. "No, vixen," he admonished and placed his hand in the middle of her torso, pushing her flat to the mattress again. "Feet flat, knees bent so I can give you what you need, what your pretty little cunt is asking for." He eased her legs down, stroking down her calf and capturing her ankle before anchoring her where he wanted her.

He rubbed the bristle of his jaw against her face and neck, branding her. She wanted to feel it on her breasts.

She'd be wearing a high-neck dress to hide the mark of his beard on her skin. He filled his hands with the aching tightness of her nipples, grazing them with his teeth into tight, tender, points. "You look like a banquet of strawberries and cream."

"You really do want me laid out on your table," she said wonderingly, suddenly shy at the admission of his weakness. The tableau he'd painted with his words earlier echoed between them. She wanted to impress him with her confidence and didn't like the shift in the balance of power. "I want to feel your fingers and tongue inside me."

"Soon enough, Impatient One. Let me sample your charms at my leisure," he chastised. His gaze intent on the thrum of his fingers against her clitoris, he scissored his middle and ring finger through her folds. "Your juicy little box is dripping...begging for my cock," he growled and lifted his fingers to his mouth. He kept his eyes avidly fixed on hers as he slowly licked them, swiping across his knuckles with a wicked tongue she knew would feel like sin incarnate delving inside her. She'd read about men doing those things, but never thought she'd experience them. All the lurid drawings she'd found in her husband's secret stash flashed through her mind.

He dropped his hand to her again, stroking her crown with his thumb and thrusting his teasing fingers through her curls. He set his palm against the rise of her vulva, and it felt like a warming pan against the bottoms of her feet on a frigid winter night. "Now, I'll make you mine," he promised and slid knuckle-deep inside her vagina, brushing against her inner walls. He dropped his body, hovering over her, and sucked her nipple into his mouth. He bit it gently and she moaned at the twin sensations of the honeyed warmth around her breast and the solid weight of his hand pressing her into the mattress. She arched into that warmth, her hands scrabbling against the sheets.

Her toes curled and she thrashed, beyond caring how much she revealed. His ministrations made her shiver and quake. "Now I'm going to taste you," he threatened.

But it didn't feel like a threat. Or sound like a threat. It was a promise. And she was on tenterhooks with the wanting of it.

He inched down and pulled her legs over his shoulders, burying his face in her quim and sinuously lapping up the evidence of her arousal. His whiskers scratched the soft skin of her inner thighs, just like he'd vowed he would do, as he laid the flat of his tongue against her clitoris. Her left foot twitched, and she could feel the tremor from his concentrated assault in her calves. He wrung every last drop from her, and when he finally slid her legs back down, she was nothing more than a puddle of brimming satisfaction and satiated curiosity.

"Did the maids exaggerate my abilities?"

She turned to her side, so she faced him. She couldn't stop the spread of a soft smile, and she wagered he deserved it. "They did not.

You've given me memories I can savor again and again on long, cold winter nights."

He tenderly brushed the damp tendrils of hair from her brow. "I plan to give you as many as I can while we're cocooned together in the aftermath of this blizzard, safe from prying eyes."

She'd only meant to indulge her fantasies this one night. To experience the thrill of bed sport with a skilled, generous partner who was confident enough to give her what she asked for and let her take what she needed. She hadn't bargained on feeling an immediate sense of loss at the thought of only one night with this man. She hadn't bargained on mutual respect and reciprocity, and what it would be like to lie beside him on a soft mattress in front of a warm hearth, his hand tangled with hers. She hadn't bargained on him falling into a deep, contented sleep, or feeling safer than she'd felt in years. So safe her mind was quiet, and her thoughts weren't skittering in twenty different directions as she considered ifs and whens.

She slipped from the bed and grabbed one of the cloths warming on the rack in front of the tub. She dipped it into the bucket and knelt beside him on the bed once again. And she stroked it over his body with a firm hand, soaking up his sweat and his essence. He stirred beneath her touch, his eyes drowsy and half-lidded. "Come here, vixen," he pleaded in a gritty voice, and pulled her down, so her head was resting on his chest and their legs were tangled together. She snuggled into his embrace as he stroked her hair and drifted to sleep with the scent of their intimacy surrounding her.

***

They'd both slept like it was a night of too much whiskey consumption. Limbs entwined around each other in impossible acrobatic contortions that should've prevented deep slumber but instead encouraged it. There'd been no bathing and no repeat performances. When she finally rose from the tangle of sheets, it was midmorning. She was alone, but the pillow beside her carried the indentation of his head.

She needed to take a bath, even though the water in the buckets was cold. She was approaching them with trepidation, bracing herself for an encounter she was sure would remind her of a dip into the lake in early spring, when there was a light rap on the door.

She reached for the sheet and wrapped it around her body. "Come in," she called out.

It was him. "I came up here to retrieve the buckets and refill them. The copper pan is heating against the brazier now and I've retrieved one of Rachel's gowns from the attic for you to don." He cleared his throat. "It may be tight across your bosom."

She wanted to giggle at his consternation. Apparently, she was more well-endowed than Rachel had been. "Thank you," she replied. "I wasn't looking forward to a cold bath."

"I didn't want you to suffer for our distraction last night," he replied with a wink and a mischievous grin. "I thought you'd be awake and alert," he ran his hand through his hair, so it fell over his face in waves, reminding her of the way he'd been at her mercy last night when she'd pulled it from his queue and sifted through the strands of inky silk. "But now you're standing here in front of me with nothing between us but a sheet and my swiftly evaporating self-control," his eyes devoured her, the forest green gleaming darker than his hair. "My thoughts and my will are scattered by the rumpled waterfall that ends above the generous curve of your ass, and the satisfaction I see reflected in your eyes," his words faded to a low rumble.

"The girls will be awake soon," she countered, reluctantly reminding him that their time was not their own.

"That knowledge is the only thing keeping me from tossing you back onto the bed. And it's a barely there, tenuous acknowledgment. I could easily be convinced to cast it aside in favor of more delectable morning activities," he confessed with a rueful smile.

"I promise to keep the sheet on, so I don't tempt you into wayward morning antics."

"I'm determined to pretend you're wearing ten thousand layers and carry on with the task at hand instead of bending you over the chair," he growled.

He hefted the buckets and headed for the door. He'd nearly convinced her of his success when he reached the threshold. He half-twisted his body towards her, the buckets sloshing water onto the floor. "You need to wash fast, vixen, or I'll be tempted to join you. The rest of my plans for the day be damned."

For the first time since she'd turned twelve, she giggled.

Ten minutes later she heard him thumping up the stairs again. "I don't trust myself to bring these in without ravishing you on the spot."

"So you still can't control your cock around me," she smugly observed through the barricade of the door.

He snorted and pushed open the door, carefully placing the full pails just inside the threshold. He reached out and grasped the edge of the sheet clasped under her armpits, and used it to tug her closer. "I haven't been able to do that since you woke up snuggled in my arms with straw in your hair."

"You flatter my vanity."

"You're the most enticing, intriguing woman I've ever met. But I digress. Is there anything else you need before I head to the stables to check on the mares who are due to foal?"

"What are your plans for the day? I'm going to suggest building a snowman to the girls."

"I don't think they've ever done that," he clicked his tongue against the roof of his mouth. "And that's no one's fault but mine. I'm sure my daughters would love that immeasurably. Especially the twins."

"I promise to bundle them up so they won't feel the cold."

He kissed the top of her head. "I trust you with the lights of my life, Arie."

Her heart skipped a beat. Did she want that trust? He gave it to her so freely – what did that mean? She gulped, and eked out, "We'll be careful."

He gave her a soft smile. "I have no doubts."

As he strode away she wanted to open her hands. They felt so full. Of the world. Of possibility. Of things she couldn't make hers. It felt as if he'd laid his beating heart in her palms.

Bright Copper Kettles (And Tubs)

Try as he might, he couldn't feel guilty about touching her last night. About letting her touch him. Even now, as he was kneeling in the hay, stroking the sides of the laboring mare, his thoughts turned to the way she'd felt snuggled in his arms. The smoldering embers in her gaze when she swaggered away after making him lose his mind. The confidence he'd given her when she'd straddled him.

He'd woken from a restful slumber free of the screams and cannon fire. Only the second one he'd had in over six and a half years.

She claimed she wasn't a suitable match. That she had neither the position nor the inclination. Though he acknowledged why she thought she wasn't in a situation that allowed her to accept an honest offer, he refused to accept her reasoning. The storm was the worst they'd had in twenty years or more, and they'd be cocooned against the world for at least another five days. He was determined to use them productively. He was going to make it his mission to convince her St. Simon House was where she belonged. At his side and in his bed.

He'd loved his wife, but they'd grown up together. Their marriage had always been an assumed eventuality. Inevitable because their families had been close, and they'd always existed in each other's shadow. When their experimentation had resulted in Rachel's pregnancy, they'd mutually agreed to marry. They had been both a surety and a comfort to one another. While he'd enjoyed the occasional tryst since his return from the Crimea, none of his partners had made him dream of more. They'd had their own agendas and were only interested in a sensual interlude. A delusion he'd thought he wanted as well. Until the woman he left standing in the doorway just now peered drowsily up at him with straw in her hair. Since their encounter in the stable, he'd embraced the possibility of a life that might be richer and fuller than the one he'd relegated himself to.

He didn't want to let her go when the snow started to melt. He didn't want her to return to the petty rule of her stepson. To people who didn't appreciate her or see her worth. To those who loved nothing more than exerting their dominance and ensuring her submission to their will because they confined her to a life without choices. She deserved so much more. She deserved sunlight and freedom. She deserved the right to speak her mind without fear of repercussion. To run barefoot through the meadows chasing butterflies.

He could give her all those things. Offer them to her. Perchance that offer would include the heart he thought no woman would ever be able to touch again.

He wanted to wake up beside her every morning. To see the wave of her hair across his pillow, her arms flung across his chest and their legs tangled together.

The mare's sides heaved beneath his hand, and he cooed softly. She grunted and the foal slipped to the straw. He let go as she staggered to her feet and twisted around to nuzzle the new arrival and clean it.

The new addition was a chestnut filly with a blaze down the middle of her snout and the longest lashes he'd ever seen. She whickered softly as her dam cleaned her, and Thaddeus immediately wanted to share his wonder with Arie.

This was one of the things he loved the most about being a steward of the land and its creatures. Welcoming new life into the world, ensuring everyone and everything under his care had the best beginning he could give them.

This filly with her bright eyes and shiny coat would be the perfect gift for his guest. A way to heal her heart from the sale of the mare she'd obviously loved so much. He'd seen the hurt she tried to hide when she spoke of the way they'd been parted. Her resignation to one more thing that had been ripped away from her.

He'd already purchased a new Dartmoor pony for the twins – a roan gelding with a cream-colored mane and tail. The horse trader was due tomorrow. And he'd already promised to give Ruby and Pearl riding lessons. Even if Arie was stubborn enough to continue refusing him, he could at least insist she accompany her charges to those lessons. He'd chip away at her resolve one chaperoned visit at a time.

He knew better than to present her with the filly at Greaves Manor. Hugh would be grievously affronted and would either forbid her from further association or simply add the mount to his own stables and commandeer its use for his own pleasure. No, it was better that Thad simply keep the horse here, feed it and care for it. An enticement for her to visit whenever she could spare the time if his efforts to convince her she belonged permanently at his side failed.

He made sure the pair had plenty of water and fresh straw before making his way toward the house. As much as he wanted to immediately seek her out, he needed a bath first. He warmed the buckets himself and set the tub up in front of the kitchen stove. It was convenient and cozy and Betty had already headed back to the smithy for the evening. There was already a pot of stew hanging from the crook suspended over the embers and the sun had sunk below the horizon hours ago. He wouldn't be interrupted.

He'd just closed his eyes and reclined his head against the back, letting the steaming water lap over his sore muscles, when the door creaked open. He watched through a slitted gaze as the woman who'd been occupying his thoughts for the entire afternoon crept toward the stove in the corner. She lifted the teapot from the eye that was its permanent resting place, and he heard her sigh in pleasure when she noted it was still hot. He was hidden from view by the large wooden table, and he stayed quiet. Content to watch her puttering about like Mother Hubbard.

When she'd poured the hot water over a scoop of loose tea, he cleared his throat. "You could join me once you finish drinking that," he rumbled.

She jumped in surprise and nearly dropped the tin cup cradled in her palms. Her bewildered expression was nearly identical to the one she'd given him when she woke up in his arms in the stables. "I didn't see you," she hoarsely admitted as her gaze skated over him and dipped to his waistline. The soap bubbles were rapidly disappearing and wouldn't hide his reaction to her presence for much longer.

"I delivered a foal today, and needed to wash away the barn and ease my sore muscles," he explained.

She plastered a bright smile on her face and kept her gaze firmly away from his body. "So the birth went well?"

"Exceedingly. A chestnut filly with a blaze and two white socks made her debut."

"How wonderful," she wistfully observed.

"She'll make an enviable plow horse if she shares her dam's conformation and spirit."

"So you intend to sell her to one of the other landowners?"

"I'm not certain. I'm sure she'll catch the eye of someone at the auction."

"You don't intend to keep her?" Her question was full of dismay.

"No." Now wasn't the time to show his hand.

"I can't fault you," she sighed. "You have a farm to run. I'd love to pay a visit to the new arrival tomorrow, though, if you can spare the time."

He winked. "I'll always spare the time for you, Vixen."

Her eyes widened and she put her finger to her lips. "Hush!" she admonished. "We shouldn't be so familiar outside the bed chamber. Especially when you're sitting there naked as the day you were born."

"My offer to join me still stands."

"We'll be caught in flagrante delicto."

"Not if we're careful. Not if you lock the door. I missed supper and I know the girls are abed. Your delicate sensibilities didn't prevent you from tying me to a chair or greeting me naked at your door," he pointed out. "So why let them win now? Why should you allow your dignity to get in the way of your bliss?"

His words curled around her, a velvety promise. She shrugged and turned to the door. She latched it and turned back toward him.

One of his hands rose from the water and he held it up, his palm an open invitation.

He looked like a reclining satyr, his body sprawled elegantly over the rounded edges of the tub. He'd leaned his head against the back, and his arms and knees extended over the sides. He was the very picture of temptation. More than a satyr. More like Dionysus encouraging her to cast away all her cares and inhibitions and sink into him like a passionate, bacchanalian adventure.

She didn't spare a single moment to question the wisdom of joining him. She wanted more than the thorough, but brief, interlude she'd enjoyed last night. She toed off her slippers and pulled the soft cotton of her borrowed night rail over her head. She gingerly crept forward and came to a halt at the side of the tub, slipping her hand into his palm.

The fire in his pale green eyes could have easily incinerated her where she stood. She shifted restlessly, feeling pinned by the intensity of that gaze. She lifted her hands in a half-hearted attempt to evade the hunger emanating from him like a tidal wave. He slowly shook his head back and forth.

He tugged her forward gently, until she was mere seconds from toppling over him. "You never have a reason to hide from me, Arie." His assurance was reverent and soothing.

"I am not in the first blush of youth, and the kitchen is more well-lit than the bedchamber."

"If I wanted a girl instead of a woman, I'd be tupping the tavern keeper's daughter. I want you, with all your gorgeous curves that show you live your life as you please and claim your joy whenever you can. I want you with the lines of laughter fanning from the corners of your smoke whiskey eyes like starlight," he finished quietly, his fingertips tracing the contours of her face.

If his touch hadn't lodged in her heart like a simmering promise, his words would have. The combination of his touch and assurance was all the encouragement she needed to make her decision. She tumbled over the side of the tub and landed in his lap. The water splashed onto the floor, and he anchored her against him, his broad hands spanning the entire circle of her waist.

His chameleon eyes sparkled with laughter and her heart toppled headlong, arse over teakettle, just as her body had done moments before. His teasing, playful treatment was a hook in her main artery. His conscientious, provocative wheedling was a permanent tattoo against her skin. When the blackthorn winter wind stopped howling at the door and there was only the memory of snow now piled on the threshold, she would cherish these bright moments of joy.

Every inch of her skin was wet. The aftermath of his invitation dripped from the ends of her hair, slid down her body in cold rivulets. He tipped his head forward and lapped at the pool of water trapped in the hollow of her throat. His tongue followed the path of his mouth, and then his hands as he brushed the stray drops from her shoulders and the crevices behind her ears.

She moaned when his teeth gnawed on the tip of her earlobe, when his whisper sawed against the edge of her jaw, "Rest easy, vixen."

The metal of the tub was unforgiving against her knees, and she shifted to ease the pressure. Her core brushed against his erection and they both groaned at the contact.

He feathered kisses along her jawline and nipped the taut muscles of her neck. She skated her hands over the bronzed slope of his shoulders and the biceps that flexed as he held her against him.

Thaddeus dropped his hand beneath the water, and Arie arched to meet his touch. Those clever hands and dexterous fingers she could never tear her gaze from brushed through her folds before tweaking her clit. He swallowed her response with his kiss as he stroked her there, where she was wet from water and arousal.

She felt the broad head of his cock swelling beneath her and slid forward. He slid into her and threw his head back. "Put your hands on my shoulders, Vixen, and brace yourself," he rumbled.

She rose from her knees and met his thrust with her body. His hands landed on her hips, and he controlled the pace with calculated determination. When Arie tightened her muscles around the length of his cock, he shuddered and bent forward. He set the edge of his teeth against her shoulder, marking her. She arched her back and he dipped his head to her chest. His tongue and teeth rasped her beaded nipples, the bristle around his mouth and on his cheeks after a long day a welcome abrasion that made them rosy and swollen.

The pace was relentless and overwhelming, and she could feel every hard inch of him sliding into her. His sleek invasion turned her body into nothing more than an instrument of pleasure, one he strummed and coaxed with undeniable expertise. She was a harp in his hands and his mouth, and he plied her just as he would the strings. He knew exactly which chords to pluck and caress. He knew how to compose a symphony that shimmered through her veins like lightning.

"Are you with me, sweet Arie?" he grated.

"I could be nowhere else," she sighed.

She sank down as he hammered upward, and they both gasped at the rush of warmth.

She reveled in the release of his seed within her.

"You're on the verge, love, let me bring you all the way there," he murmured, half-hard inside her.

He slipped his hand between them again, thumbing her clitoris in a steady rhythm as the water lapped around them. She tipped her head forward to watch him stroke her.

"Pinch those blushing nipples for me, and you'll fall off the edge."

She obeyed him and felt the rush of her own release moments later. It scoured her like the tide on the sands, leaving her wrung out and boneless.

"You didn't pull away this time either," she murmured as she dropped her head to his shoulder.

"Nay, lass, I didn't. But you'll knock on my door if your womb quickens with my seed."

"I doubt it will. Ten years of being plowed by my husband, remember?" she sleepily reminded him.

"A man three times your age. 'Tis far more likely the fault was his, not yours."

"If there are consequences, I'll tell you." She promised. "Although I think your worries are unfounded."

"Whether they are unfounded or not, they are there. If there's the ghost of a chance I can make you mine for longer than this brief arrangement, even if it's through coercion, I'll take advantage of the opportunity."

She didn't hear his declaration because she'd fallen fast asleep in his arms.

WARM WOOLEN MITTENS

Her host hadn't exactly condoned the day's activities, and she didn't know how the results would be received. But she wasn't going to allow it to deter her.

"Papa forbade us from pestering the servants," mumbled Rissa.

"What do you mean? Pestering them how?" she asked.

"He said the Christmas spirit has nothing to do with trees or greenery or chimneys. I think it's because of Mama and our brothers, though." Clementine explained.

"I know what's it's like to miss your mother."

Callie slipped her hand into Arie's. "It helps us when Clem tells us stories about her. We were only three years old when she died and we don't remember very much."

"Papa told us you lost your mother too."

If her story helped ease their pain and made the holiday easier, there was no harm in sharing it. Even if the memories were painful. "I was nine years old when my mother collapsed into a heap in the middle of the garden. I was helping her weed the row of lettuce, and when I started screaming, my father came running. He carried her to the second-floor bedroom and that's where she lived until she died." Her mother was confined there for the next two and a half years, and all of the responsibility of taking care of the household and her younger siblings fell on Arie's slight, scrawny shoulders.

The woman who'd been the thread binding their family together had hovered on an agonizing precipice between life and death and a month before Arie turned twelve, she slipped away. Arie was squeezing her hand the entire time, immovable from her bedside.

"I wish I could've held my mama's hand," Clem quietly confessed.

Arie pulled her into a hug. "I'm sure she knew how much you loved her. And I know she loved all of you with her whole heart. "

"Papa's been sad too. And I think he blames himself. I remember him reading A Christmas Carol to all of us, but he hasn't done it since everyone died."

"I was scared of the ghosts." Callie somberly informed her.

"The Christmas spirit is a feeling of good will and inner peace. A willingness to forgive the foibles of your comrades, and let strangers enjoy the warmth of your hearth and the bounty of your table. A time to let bygones be bygones. But it's a lot easier to be inclined toward feeling those things if you're celebrating. Do you think we should ask your papa to read it to us tonight?"

"If we decorate the house, will that make Papa more inclined?" interjected Callie.

"Yes," answered Ruby before Arie had a chance to explain. Over the last three days she'd set aside her often sullen behavior and blossomed into a slightly pretentious mother hen, helping Clem shepherd the younger girls around the house like porcelain dolls she was afraid the world was going to knock off a shelf.

"How do you know? He's not your papa." Claire challenged.

Ruby knelt and took the youngest girl's hands in her own. "I know because he's nothing like my papa. He isn't afraid to show you how much he loves you, and I think if we decorate he'll remember how special those holidays were and wonder why your family stopped celebrating that way."

"Is that true, Arie?' The little girl asked, biting her lip.

"I think it might be true." She didn't know how Thaddeus was going to react to their efforts, and she didn't want to give his daughters false hope.

"But pine boughs stink," protested Rissa, wrinkling her pert freckled nose in disgust.

"They don't stink!" Callie corrected her sister. "It smells like the outside, and the hill we used to sleigh down with our brothers when we were little. Before Mama died."

The twins shared a sad smile and joined their pinkies.

Rissa turned to Arie. "Arie, if Papa says no to decorating, do you think he'll let us go sledding instead?'

"He won't have the chance to say no- because we're not asking him are we, Arie?" asked Clem with narrowed eyes.

"It's better to ask for forgiveness than permission, that's what Arie always tells us when she wants to teach us something she doesn't think our mother will approve of."

Pearl once again demonstrated her insight into the motives of the people around her. She was the most precocious child Arie had ever met. "Yes, Pearl. You're correct. We aren't asking for permission. We're going to take matters into our own hands and ask for forgiveness instead."

Thaddeus's daughters' eyes became round as saucers. "Papa won't like it," they warned in unison.

Arie shrugged. "Let me worry about that."

"Can we still go sledding?" pleaded Rissa.

She fondly rumpled the girl's curls. "Of course," she assured her. "As soon as we've chosen the tree and the greenery, we'll go sledding."

"Hooray!" clapped the four younger girls. "We loved building the snowman with you, Arie."

After Thaddeus had knocked on her door yesterday morning, given his regrets he wouldn't be able to join them and dropped a kiss on her forehead, she and the girls had spent yesterday chasing each other about. And then she'd taught them how to build a snowman. They'd filched walnuts from the pantry for the eyes, and a wizened carrot stub for the nose. The head groom had given them a corncob pipe destined for the midden heap, and Pearl had contributed a handful of shiny pebbles that were buried in the pocket of her skirt. They'd built him just to the left of the wide front door, and Thaddeus's bright smile at the sight of the new sentry had immensely gratified her. He'd put his arm around her waist, reeled her in, and kissed the top of her head.

They'd played a game of charades in front of the fire that night, before retiring. He'd spent the day chopping firewood and mending fences, and she could see the lines of exhaustion in his face. He'd fallen asleep to her vigorously rubbing his shoulders as he groaned in appreciation and then fell silent. Fifteen minutes later he was snoring contentedly. She'd sifted her hands through the waves of his hair, snuggled into the warmth of his side and drifted off.

One of the grooms had rapped on the door this morning just before dawn and slid a note across the threshold. One of the prize ewes Thaddeus had been fretting over had started a difficult labor in the middle of the night. He'd thrown on his clothes, kissed her on the forehead, and headed out. She'd known his brow was creased and his shoulders were tight with worry. The roads were still impassable, and neither the vet nor the farrier would be able to reach them. She knew he had an advanced knowledge of husbandry that would stand him in good stead, but she wanted to do something to cheer him up in the event something went wrong.

He hadn't exactly prohibited them from celebrating the holiday. When she'd broached the possibility of making the hall and the parlor more festive he'd responded with, "We haven't decorated since Rachel's death. She embraced all the new royal traditions as if they were her own. Even the ridiculous notion of Santa Claus squeezing down the chimney from that Clement Moore poem. Decorating again would remind us of her death. It would remind me of my lapse in judgment, and my choice to go to war instead of remaining here."

While Arie respected how he felt, she believed he'd change his mind once he saw how the holiday fanfare transformed the house into something bordering the magical and made his daughters smile. She was convinced they were all in need of a reminder that the holidays were meant to celebrate blessings and new beginnings.

***

The forester helped them find a tree and he and two of the farmhands loaded the cart full of boughs. Once a prime spot had been chosen for the display, she'd held fast to her promise. She was trudging up the hill, pulling the sleigh behind her, winded, her cheeks red with cold and her legs like blocks of lead, when she saw him approaching them. She couldn't read his expression from this far away, but his pace was so thunderous, she'd wager it matched his glower. She pulled the sleigh to a halt at the top. "Girls, why don't you have a bit of a snowball fight?" she urged as his determined strides ate up the space between them. His head was bare and she wanted to scold him for being out in the weather without a scarf. But scolding was something that rose from affection. And even though he'd made a pseudo offer of marriage when she'd first arrived, affection beyond the physical enjoyment of each other's bodies had no place between them.

Arie shoved away the irrational need to chastise him for leaving his ears vulnerable to the elements and whirled around, braced for impact.

A sharp burst of laughter from one of the girls distracted her, and she turned to watch them pelt toward the edge of the clearing and the shelter of trees at its edge. She was turning toward him again, confident in Ruby and Clementine's ability to watch over the younger girls, when his leather glove curled around her upper arm.

"I want to hold onto my anger," he growled. "But you make it impossible. You've brought light into the holidays again. My daughters are laughing and smiling more than they have in longer than I can remember," he ran his other hand through his hair, the friction of the glove disheveling it with a crackle. "Explain why your motives for going against my wishes were completely pure."

"I thought it would help," she placed her mittened hand in the middle of his chest. "The twins told me they remembered sleigh rides with their brothers and Clem remembers the scent of pine and your readings of Dickens. I just wanted the girls to remember a piece of their mother untainted by grief. It's something I wish someone had done for me."

He sighed. "My intention was never to make them feel like they should forget what they've lost. I was just trying to spare all of us the burden of additional pain. You were right to run roughshod over my misgivings, even if it provoked me," he admitted. "But that doesn't mean you're completely forgiven for your audacity and deciding that asking for forgiveness was the right course of action when I wasn't as enthusiastic about your proposition as you wanted me to be. It was tantamount to disobedience and you shouldn't think you'll escape punishment later. You purposefully ignored my sentiments."

Her blood heated at the look in his eyes. "My punishment later?" she fluttered her lashes and tapped her finger against his shoulder.

He slowly peeled the glove from his right hand, easing the tight leather over his fingers one knuckle at a time. The display was so full of calculated, yet raw, masculine strength and presumption she couldn't look away. "I believe cravats are highly underrated instruments of sensual torture, and I can think of many inventive uses that transcend knotting one around my neck. It makes me exceedingly happy I haven't adopted the use of neck ties. A cravat is so much more voluminous," he slid his bare finger down the bridge of her nose. "Your instigation of our drapery cord adventure is long overdue for a payback."

"Is that a threat or a promise?" She breathily challenged.

"I think turnabout is fair play and you're the one who'll be trussed up tonight. So consider it what you will," he enigmatically replied.

"Those rules only apply to things like chess and five card loo," she scoffed.

"We can make wagers, just as we would across the chess board or a gaming table," he waggled his brows suggestively.

"What would we wager? I don't have any coin to spare." She buffed her nails against the wool of his jacket and then casually exhaled across her fingertips, goading him to accept her barely concealed dare.

"You'd like to test your skills against mine?"

"I would."

"I think the cravat and other things could be used to invigorate the competition. But first I think you're entitled to a downhill sleigh ride."

"The girls and I have been wearing a path in the snow since just after breakfast."

"But you haven't ridden with me – I've had many years to hone my steering abilities and you'll be the beneficiary of all that expertise. It's just as expansive as those skills I demonstrated the other night," he lightly caressed the inner skin of her wrist. "And I promise to haul us back to the top afterwards."

His low tone insinuated he was referring to steering abilities that had nothing to do with a sled. He dropped her hand and strode toward the children. "Who of you is in favor of a bit of chocolate in front of the fire?"

She watched bemusedly as they started jumping up and down in excitement. "Nan never lets us have it!" Rissa squealed as she threw herself into her father's arms.

He smiled down at the more outgoing twin, and even though she couldn't discern details from this distance, she imagined the crinkles at the corners of his eyes and the pop of the dimple bracketing his mouth as he grinned down at his boisterous daughters.

"Really, Papa?" squeaked Claire. "It's not too dear?"

He reached out to tousle the curls trailing from the confines of her knitted cap. "No, poppet. It's not too dear."

She didn't want to interrupt the tender moment, but he stretched his hand in her direction, beckoning her to his side with the crook of one finger. "I'm going to take a trip down the hill with Ms. Arie."

She reached them in time to see their eyes widen in delight. "She needs a turn," Clem solemnly informed him. "She's been hauling us to the top after every ride. And the snow is so deep, your boots get stuck in it."

"I landed on a little stone when we toppled out, Papa." Claire chimed in. "She kissed it better and carried me back to the top of the hill."

"Then I think we can all agree it's her turn to have some fun as well."

Fun was a word as foreign to Arie as love. Becoming a surrogate mother to her sisters at the age of twelve meant she'd had to let go of her childhood early. The prospect of soaring down a blanket of pristine snow, of being briefly airborne in the arms of this man, made her heart stutter in her chest. She blinked hard, patting her cheeks and stomping her feet in a futile attempt to quell the tide of tears rising in her throat.

He gently set Rissa on the ground. "It will be your job to cheer us on." He may as well have given them crowns and appointed them protectors of the realm. They all clasped their hands in front of them and acknowledged the assignment with enthusiastic nods.

Arie crept forward, and finally slid her hand into the clasp extended toward her.

He gestured toward the sleek wooden sled. "Have a seat, Your Majesty," he commanded as he gave her a sweeping bow.

This one was far more elaborate than the one he'd given her in the stable. He bent so far at the waist, his nose nearly touched the snowy ground, and the flourish of his arm was worthy of the obeisance one would show a sultan or the Queen herself. The girls giggled rowdily at his display.

She gingerly sat on the device that would soon become a flying carpet. He clambered behind her, grasping the rope in his solid grip. His body surrounded her, the faint scent of seasoned hay and the tang of his sweat in her nostrils. His arms bracketed her from behind, their pose somehow more intimate than the sight of him kneeling between her knees had been.

"Are you ready, Your Majesty?" he rumbled into her hair.

The rough, teasing edge to his voice burrowed beneath her skin like the syrup from a treacle tart. Slightly decadent, with the sharp bite of chocolate and the tart zest of lemon. She couldn't push words past the knot in her chest or the lump in her throat. She nodded in response.

Somehow he sensed how much the experience was affecting her. He didn't ask questions or try to deflect the weight of her feelings. He tenderly brushed the hair that had slid from the tidy bun at her nape away from her shoulders. "I've got you, vixen," he whispered.

And the lump in her throat almost choked her. No one had ever had her.

He pushed them off with a shout of "Huzzah!" She dimly heard the girls shouting with excitement through the roar in her ears. She gripped his arms with a strength she didn't even know she possessed.

They flew over the knoll at the halfway point, suspended in the air for a brief second that felt like a lifetime. She wanted to spread makeshift wings like Icarus, tilting her face towards the sun. She couldn't hold in her shriek of delight.

They landed with a hard thump at the bottom, and the runners skidded over the edge of a rock. The jolt unceremoniously dumped them into the snow and suddenly she was sprawled over his warm, laughing expanse, tears finally coursing down her cheeks. She still felt the throb of sorrow, but was grateful he'd had the foresight to give her this glimpse of a carefree childhood. Her tears were an expression of that. She was so grateful she'd met this man who had already given her so many sparkling moments.

He brushed the tears away with his bared hand, cupped her cheek and burrowed his fingers into what was left of the tightly wound bun at the nape of her neck. His gaze was wary because he was hyper aware of the fragility beneath the mask of calm competency she presented to the world. He exerted gentle pressure, until their noses were nestled against each other and the only flimsy barrier to a full embrace was the sharp dig of her bony elbows propped against his chest.

Her eyes brightened again with the sheen of unshed tears, and the mid-afternoon sun caught them, so they looked like fractured prisms.

She leveraged herself up, bracing a hand on his chest so she could rest on his haunches. She could feel the damp ground seeping through the wool of her gown and stockings, and the frogs of her cloak had come undone when they tumbled into a heap. He pressed his thumb against the pulse fluttering in the hollow juncture of her throat.

His hand tipped her chin down, and the cold velvet of his touch was like the unexpected prick of an embroidery needle on the pad of her finger. His leather and brimstone scent surrounded her, and she angled deeper into his embrace, her inner thighs brushing against his arousal. His eyes narrowed and he hissed as he swiveled his hips, dragging himself against her.

"Is Arie hurt, Papa?" Rissa's shrill voice interrupted their reverie. They blinked in unison, slowly emerging from the cocoon of deceptive warmth they'd built between the shift of their bodies.

He dropped his hand from her face and cleared his throat to respond. "No, poppet, she's not." He lifted her from his lap with a firm grip on her hips and she hopped up, brushing her skirt free of snow. "But I think she lost her mittens," he called out. "And I lost my self-control," he muttered. "Thank goodness the cold will make short work of this," he observed, gesturing between them toward the very noticeable rise and twitch of his cock. He clambered up as well and bent toward her. "Let me," he coaxed and focused his attention on refastening her cloak. He turned away to scour their landing spot for her scarlet mittens.

"There they are," she pointed to the swell midway up the hill.

"We'll fetch them on the way up," he assured her and tugged her behind him. He scooped them up, and when he handed them to her she decided she'd brave frostbite rather than abandon the way her entire palm was enveloped in his.

She was subdued during the walk back to the house, even though the girls were cavorting around her. He was a silent guardian at her side, his pinky finger occasionally brushing her own where it swung at her side. That infinitesimal touch sent a racing frisson of awareness spiraling down her spine, until it was a lump of anticipation and yearning and confusion in the pit of her stomach.

She could feel the banked tension emanating from his body. She wanted to yank him behind the paddocks and push him down in front of her. She wanted to brace her hands on his shoulders, sling her legs over the broad breadth of his back, hook her ankles behind his neck and order him to taste her again. The memory of his tongue made her squirm beneath the layers of wool.

A Heart Suddenly Touched

The warmth of the kitchen enveloped them, and Thad watched with bemusement as Arie seated herself on the floor and wrested the girls' boots off. "Now, go stretch your legs in front of the hearth in the sitting room and I'll make us all a pot of chocolate." She directed them.

He'd sat on the stool to remove his own boots, and realized one of his socks had a hole big enough for his toe to poke through. No wonder it had felt like someone was driving an icepick into that shoe as they'd trudged back home. He swiftly tucked it under the stool.

"There's no use hiding it."

"I'm not hiding anything." Did the infernal woman have eyes in the back of her head? Her back had been turned as she placed the girls' footwear on the hearth to dry.

"You're a single father and I'm certain your socks need darned because you think of everyone else's needs before your own. Hand it over." She tilted her open palm in his direction.

"You're here as our guest. You're not meant to mend my garments." He hoped he sounded commanding and not petulant.

She planted her hands on her hips and sighed in the direction of the ceiling. Which was a good indication he sounded petulant.

"How else will I spend my time? We've stew enough to last at least two days, the laundry can wait, and the girls have been entertaining themselves with minimal supervision."

"You're not going to let me refuse, are you?"

"No, I'm not. You're being ridiculous."

"I'm not being ridiculous. You're here as my guest and I'm not letting you darn my socks."

"I'm not going to argue about this with you." She dropped to the floor at his feet and tugged the leg toward her he'd tried to hide from view.

Her fingers felt like little anvils prickling with heat against his skin as she rolled down the garment that had offended her.

"I'm only letting you do this because if I don't, you'll never let me hear the end of it."

She harrumphed. "And you dared accuse me of being the stubborn one."

He felt more naked than he should with one bare foot. Even more exposed than he'd felt during their encounter in her bedchamber or their sojourn in the tub. He was keenly aware that she had somehow wrested control of the situation, and highlighted the vulnerability he wanted to hide from the world.

"You are the stubbornest woman I've ever met." He insisted with a grumble. "Most women would've taken no for an answer and wouldn't have removed my sock."

She threw him an indiscernible look over her shoulder as she draped the sock over the arm of the chair. "You should question the motives and suitability of any woman who takes no for an answer. She likely has neither the desire nor the aptitude to care for your household."

"So instead I should seek out a woman who commandeers the situation despite my misgivings?"

"I've already informed you that's exactly the type of woman your marriage prospects should include."

"What if I've already found her?"

"What if she's exasperated by your refusal to accept her decision?"

He shrugged. "It's not a refusal to accept her decision. It's simply a cotton headed belief in my ability to persuade her otherwise."

"It's not a matter of persuasion. It's a matter of responsibility. If she were free to choose her bliss over aught else, there would be no decision to make."

"I've repeatedly asked her to share her confidences with me, and she's refused that as well."

"Mayhap she's far too accustomed to keeping them to herself for fear of overburdening others."

"Mayhap I consider that fear completely unjustified and ludicrous in the extreme."

"Mayhap she's weary of the male species explaining to her exactly what her choices should entail."

"Mayhap I believe she's limiting those choices unnecessarily out of a misbegotten assessment of her situation."

"Mayhap you don't know the entirety of the situation and everything it entails."

"I have no way of knowing those things unless she tells me. Which she refuses to do." He arched a brow and crossed his arms over his chest.

Her mouth thinned into a mutinous line and she crossed her arms too. "How many times must we discuss this? Stop badgering me."

He met her slitted gaze with amusement. "But I like badgering you. I find it enervating."

"I don't find it enervating. I find it irritating. Just what are you determined to prove?"

"I attempt to prove nothing. I don't need to. You'll have an epiphany sooner or later. And when you do, I'll be right there."

"Right there for what reason?"

"To pick up the pieces, of course. You'll be at sixes and sevens when you finally realize the world is your oyster."

She rolled her eyes. "The world will never be my oyster. I am a childless widow on the cusp of thirty-nine years. I have obligations I must uphold and I have a very narrow path constrained by breadcrumbs and false displays of obeisance that I must follow."

"Breadcrumbs and obeisance? You're not pursuing martyrdom are you?"

"I know my duty, and I'll not let this sojourn dissuade me from it."

"You are not defined by your duty."

"I am defined by my duty. Throughout the entirety of my life, it has been the only thing that defined me. Your protest to the contrary demonstrates how truly unaware you are of a woman's lot."

"You sell yourself short." He rose from the stool, uncaring that he was half shod, the bare toes of his left foot an incongruity he chose to ignore. His hand was outstretched, on the verge of cupping her cheek, when a knock on the doorframe had them springing apart.

"Thad, one of the apprentices brought over a letter." Betty minced toward them, holding a sheet of paper between her thumb and forefinger.

"Bring it here then."

When she slapped it into his palm, he recognized his mother's scrawling address. "It's from my mother." His father had been recently summoned to London and the missive he held in his hand might be about that journey. He sent up a silent prayer it didn't convey bad tidings and slid the edge of his thumbnail under the seal.

Thad,

There have been reports here in the village that you are keeping company with a widow...

I know not who she is, but as your mother I have long been aware of your fascination with Araminta Greaves. I shall hope she is not the object of your attention. You know the squire will make it all the worse for you if she is. (And her.)

Your loving mother.

"Interfering besom," he grumbled. He knew her intentions stemmed from love and loyalty, but since his wife's death she'd taken a suffocatingly enthusiastic interest in marrying him off again. She'd presented him with hand-picked candidates from three counties and been incensed when he'd refused all of them as unsuitable for one reason or another. He was grateful for the care she bestowed on her granddaughters, but he was well past the age for her to be chastising him for his choices.

Arie placed a hand on his arm. "Why are you grumbling like a bear with a thorn in its paw?"

"Because somehow my mother learned of your presence here. She doesn't approve."

"Does she disapprove of the presence of any unfettered woman here, or just me?"

"Apparently just you."

Her brow furled in confusion. "Why is my presence more abhorrent or harmful than that of any other single woman of the parish?"

He sighed and braced his hands on his hips. "Because she's well aware of the history of contention between your son in law and I."

"The history of contention?"

"We've been rivals our entire lives. I thought we'd left it behind us when I departed for Crimea. I've recently learned otherwise."

"I know about the property you want to acquire, but what else is between you?"

"He's cornered the local market and forced me to go further afield to find buyers for my wool and mutton. He threatens those who'd purchase from me with dire consequences."

"So he's a tyrant."

"He always has been. I shudder to think what petty revenge he'll take for this." He motioned between them.

"This? This is just two lonely people indulging their curiosity and need for comfort. He'll never know."

"I don't want you to become sordid fodder across every supper table in the village."

"We've been fodder before. My sisters and I bore the ridicule of the parish when my father moved in with the chandler's widow. If the fodder doesn't cast me out of my living, why do I care?"

"It could very well have that effect. My mother doesn't mention your name, but if she's aware of the possibility you might be here, others are as well."

She shrugged. "There's no use crying over spilt milk. Those who wish to think the worst will always do so. My presence here taints neither my ability to watch over those girls nor my moral rectitude."

"You don't think Hugh will claim retribution?"

"It's unlikely. Neither he nor his wife want to care for their children. And they like having an unpaid housekeeper and governess at their disposal."

"Positions you need not remain in."

"I will do as I choose. In all things. Stop meddling. If there are any repercussions, I'll deal with them."

"Fine. I'll drop the subject for now. But only because I don't trust those girls to decorate the tree alone." He held his arm out for her. "Shall we?"

"Shouldn't you don another pair of socks?"

He grinned, pulled his still clad foot up and yanked off that stocking as well. "There."

She glanced down in fascination. "Your feet will become chilled."

"Nay, the sitting room has carpet and there's a merry fire in the hearth. And besides," his lips skated over the shell of her ear. "If my feet become too cold, I'll just insist you warm them tonight."

"What makes you think I'll be close enough to warm your feet tonight?"

"Because I know you won't refuse me entry. You want to make the most of every moment. Just as I do."

"Perhaps, but your arrogance about it may make me change my mind." She sailed ahead of him.

He didn't mind. The view of her from this angle was very much to his liking.

My Heart Wants to Sing

I n the handful of minutes they'd been in the sitting room alone, the children had adorned the bottom of the tree in a ridiculous profusion of colored paper, dried fruit and furniture from their doll-house. They weren't tall enough to reach past the middle, and the decorations ended abruptly, like a property line they couldn't cross. They were challenging each other to a game of leapfrog, to see if that would lift them high enough. Arie and Thad exchanged smiles and watched their antics with amusement, occasionally sharing a glance full of shared mirth and wonder.

The tree-decorating dissolved into fits of giggling and an impromptu rendition of Jingle Bells when the branches proved too much no matter how high they managed to jump. Claire broke away and cautiously approached her father. "Papa, the errand boy from the butcher's shop said Santa wasn't real when he dropped off the delivery."

Thaddeus crouched down and grabbed her hands. "He's as real as you believe him to be, little one."

Her face brightened. "I believe he's real. And I've been very well-behaved this year," she peered up at him mischievously and it was all he could do to keep a straight face. "After all, the only reason I ever get into trouble is because I'm following Rissa and Callie around and trying to get them to stop doing whatever they're doing because I know it's naughty."

He knew this was a patent falsehood, because although Claire's rebellious streak wasn't as wide as those of her sisters, she was perfectly capable of scheming and did so quite frequently. The three of them were inseparable for many reasons. Clem was forever dragging them out of scrapes and trying to make them see reason. "I'm sure Santa's been paying attention and will reward your good behavior," he reassured her as he rumpled her curls.

"I think so too," she shook her head in agreement. "I think I deserve sweets in my stocking," she confided, and clasped her hands behind her back – the very portrait of studied innocence. "And you know peppermint is my favorite." She prodded.

Her father wasn't fooled. "You may as well go ahead and ask me."

"We want to stay up until we hear the reindeer on the roof!" She excitedly declared. "Like in the poem you read to us. We want to hear the clatter."

He was tempted to indulge her and looked to Arie for guidance. She shrugged. Of course she wasn't going to chime in with her advice. Was she punishing him for his perceived arrogance earlier? Or did she enjoy watching him squirm as he tried to navigate the manipulation of his rosy cheeked, beaming nearly seven-year-old daughter? He tended to spoil her because she had no memories of her mother and he irrationally blamed himself for that absence.

"Why not?" He capitulated. His peripheral vision showed Arie smiling broadly. Obviously amused at how easily he was wrapped around his daughter's finger.

The others must have been listening closely because they suddenly swarmed him. Ruby and Pearl hung bashfully back. "Thank you, sir," Ruby curtseyed. "We'll have wonderful stories to tell Amy when we return home."

"You may want to keep the stories confined to the nursery." Their father was a stick-in-the-mud about such things and would accuse them of being fanciful and ignorant.

"I agree with Mr. St. Simon, girls," Arie chimed in. "There's no reason for your parents to hear of your adventures." There was also the chance the girls had been more observant than she and Thad were giving them credit for.

"Papa, will you give me a piggyback ride around the tree?"

"Of course cherub." He knelt down so Claire could clamber onto his back.

As he loped around the tree, the twins skipped beside them, squealing and clamoring for a turn of their own.

Arie's heart filled with yearning, and hammered in her chest like the percussive beat of a drum.

***

As Thaddeus had predicted, Claire was the last sentry standing. After a valiant fight filled with cavernous yawning that made her jaw pop and squeak on its hinges, she succumbed to the entreaty of sleep like her companions. Once he and Arie pulled blankets snugly beneath chins, they crept out of the room.

Arie had just pushed her bedroom door open when a warm weight curled around her waist. Before she even had a chance to gasp, she found herself spun around and pressed against the wall. "Are you reneging on your challenge, madam?" A gruff voice rumbled in her ear.

"No," she whispered. She hadn't been, not really. But the easy camaraderie of the evening had felt too much like the golden dreams she used to have of sitting in front of a hearth with a child in her lap and a loving husband at her side. She was too old now to indulge in dreams like that, and she was feeling too maudlin to lie to herself about the dangerous depths of their attraction. She knew it wasn't just physical and that she'd sought him out above all others for reasons besides opportunity and convenience. In her current mood, there was a danger those confessions would slip off her tongue and taint the rest of their time together.

"You're not telling me the whole truth," he chided, sliding his nose into the nook between her ear and jaw.

"What do you think I'm hiding?" She swallowed.

He ceased his nuzzling long enough to narrow his gaze to her face. "I'm not sure," he admitted. "But I think you're having second thoughts about the nature of our dalliance."

"Not exactly," she took a deep breath, steeling herself from the inside out for the things she needed to say. The things she needed them both to believe. "I think we're letting the strength of our attraction blind us to the reality of the situation."

"And what exactly do you think the reality of our situation is?"

"I think it's temporary. I think we're deluding ourselves if we treat this as anything other than what it is – a brief interlude between two lonely people. Our loneliness is our connection."

"I suffer no delusions, Arie Greaves," he murmured into her ear, the silky, slightly rough scratch of his beard rasping against her jaw as he bent closer. "I've already informed you that if we were at liberty to choose, I'd choose you. But I don't think you'd choose me," he concluded with hard finality.

"It's not that I wouldn't choose you. It's that I can't choose you." She seethed in response. How dare he misconstrue her intentions or paint her as the villain of the story. "When I told you this couldn't be anything more than a dalliance, I meant it. My life can't be about what I want."

She knew he was going to draw away before he did it. He stepped back into the shadows, facing her across the narrow strip of carpet snaking down the hallway. He shoved his hands in his pockets and reclined against the wall with his ankles crossed. His eyes were dark, darker than the shadows that swirled in the space between them, and his silhouette loomed in front of her with deceptive nonchalance. A casual observer wouldn't see the tenuous thread tethering them to each other. Or the way they seemed to be straining in each other's direction on tip toes, white-knuckled with tension and self-denial.

"Your life could be about what you want if you weren't too afraid to lay claim to your bliss." He grimly corrected. "You won't allow me to convince you, so you need to convince yourself." He gave his head a vigorous shake, like he was trying to dislodge every single thought of her from his subconscious. "I bid you good night, madam. I hope you relish your lonely bed." His parting, jaunty salute was an incredibly aggravating punctuation as he turned on his heel and headed in the opposite direction.

She watched his figure recede until it disappeared around a corner. She stood there in the half-pool of moonlight spilling from her open door, and waited for him to turn around. She decided she'd settle for a single glance over his shoulder. That one glance would be enough to make her forget her pride and chase after him. Beg him to be patient with her. To make her feel less alone. But he didn't look back.

He made her question the wisdom and the worth of all her choices. Was her sense of obligation misguided or coin better spent elsewhere? Was she wrong to wrap the things she didn't dare dream of in an imaginary shroud and shove them below the surface where they wouldn't tempt her or lure her away? Every crevice and cranny of her heart was certain there was no higher calling than ensuring her sisters were happily married to men that valued them as more than floor scrubbers and baby makers. Her sacrifices would be worth it. Even the one she was forcing herself to make right now.

Doorbells and a Cup of Tea

He'd kept his word, and he hadn't come to her in three nights. She laid awake for hours, her mind racing, hoping he'd have a change of heart and wishing she hadn't been too proud to run after him. She woke up feeling groggy every morning, and even three cups of tea later, she still didn't feel equipped to face the world.

The girls didn't notice her reticence or lackluster energy. They bombarded her every minute of the day. It was exhausting, but she was grateful for the exhaustion. It meant she didn't have the chance to think about the other infuriatingly distant adult in the house. He disappeared outside every morning after guzzling down his black swill coffee, with nary a word to her.

It was midmorning on the fourth day since he'd left her standing in the hall when a loud banging interrupted preparations for the game of snapdragon she and the girls had been about to begin.

When Arie swung open the door it revealed one of Hugh's liveried footmen. The man looked abjectly miserable. His nose ran with the cold, and his teeth were chattering. His shoes and pants were plastered to him by the snow puddling in the foyer beneath him.

Despite his forlorn appearance, Arie recognized him. "Come inside and tell me why you're here, Ivan."

"There's no need, ma'am. I have a message from the manor for you."

"You can't deliver your message when you can barely stand, and I won't send you back out into the cold without letting you at least warm up first." She sternly reprimanded.

Ruby skidded to a halt in front of them. Pearl nearly crashed into her back. Ivan sketched a bow in their general direction.

"You have icicles coming out of both nostrils," Claire informed him with a grimace as she brought up the rear of the cluster.

"Claire, that's enough. You'd likely have them too if you had to trudge five miles in the snow. I won't allow the three of you to play snapdragon unsupervised. Ruby, hand over the bowl."

The girls all sighed in protest. The wind had been brutal, and they'd all been confined indoors. They'd been looking forward to the game all day - since Arie had promised to play it with them when they'd begged her over breakfast.

"We'll play it later. Ruby and Clem, set up tiddlywinks for Rissa, Callie and Claire."

"I hate those baby games," she heard Ruby mutter as they walked away.

Ivan followed her lead and when they got to the cozy kitchen his moan of gratitude proved her instincts had been right. She shoved him onto a stool. "Sit here and have a bowl of stew and hot tea to warm you up."

He looked longingly at the pot bubbling merrily in the hearth – like it was the equivalent of the Holy Grail. "I shouldn't. I was told to deliver my message and return in time to serve the evening meal."

"You can blame your delayed return on the condition of the roads. I'm certain it won't be that much of an exaggeration."

"I was forced to walk here. Sir Hugh didn't want to chance losing one of the horses to the treacherous ice."

"But he didn't mind putting you in danger. You'll stay until you're warn again. And that's an order."

"The roads are bad, ma'am, I agree. But the party at the manor needs all of us there to keep control of things."

"What do you mean you need to be there to help control things?" She cautiously asked as she ladled the stew.

"They've named Sir Hugh the Lord of Misrule, ma'am," he informed Arie.

Apparently the absence of his children had influenced her stepson to let go of some of his rigidity. "And the person wearing this crown is encouraging behavior his children shouldn't be witnessing?"

The footman ducked his head in embarrassment. "Aye, ma'am. All the guests are chasing each other up and down the halls in their unmentionables."

"Truthfully?" she asked in astonishment.

"Yes, ma'am. Sir Hugh asked if the girls could remain here until after Silvester."

If Hugh was the one planting rumors about her presence here, he was being his usual hypocritic self.

"You'll have to ask Mr. St. Simon. We'll be imposing on his time and space. And what about their younger sister?"

"She was dispatched to the parsonage two days ago and she'll stay there for the duration of the party."

Arie sighed in relief. The parson and his wife had daughters near Amy's age. Knowing some of the proclivities of the guests, the less exposure Amy had to them, the better. Although the household staff would have intervened as much as possible, they weren't all-seeing and there was much that could escape their notice if the guests were intent on devilry or mischief.

"Mrs. Greaves and her charges may stay as long as necessary," a voice boomed from behind her.

She couldn't stop the shiver that trickled down her spine. He'd kept his distance all morning, and hadn't even glanced at her. She'd missed the sleepy rumble of his voice as it rolled through an empty room, and the sound of his boots approaching her as he stooped to kiss her forehead. The loose, lanky stride and wide smile.

She swallowed and turned to face him. "You're certain we won't be an imposition?"

"Quite the opposite," he replied. But his smile didn't reach his eyes and there was still a brick wall between them.

"Well, there you have it," she brightly informed the shivering footman. "Once you've warmed up and your teeth are no longer chattering, you can inform your master we'll be fine until we receive a summons notifying us it's safe to return."

Ivan gave her a sheepish smile. "Many thanks, ma'am. I think my feet are frozen solid in my shoes."

The man gingerly flexed his feet, favoring them as if they were icicles like the ones that had been dangling from his nostrils above his mustache when he arrived. "You may already be frostbitten. I'll send someone in to warm some water for your feet."

She bustled away, Thaddeus on her heels. When they were out of hearing range, Thaddeus broke the silence that had been lingering between them like a boulder on her chest. "You certainly took command of the situation," he commented in amusement. "Since when is broth at the ready in the kitchens? Betty never quite manages it."

She blushed, twisting her hands in the skirt of her gown. "Since I made it this morning," she confessed. "It's been simmering over the hearth since you went to the stables. I didn't know what you intended for the day or when you'd be returning, and I wanted to make sure there was something to warm your belly."

"So the broth is solely for my benefit?"

"I haven't seen much of you, and I know you've been shoveling down meals at odd hours."

He moved closer, until he was crowding her against the wall. "I didn't want to stay away. But I thought it best if we are going to maintain any semblance of control."

"I'm not that susceptible to your charms," she huffed.

He braced his hand on the narrow space of wall between her head and the entryway to the parlor. "It's not you I'm worried about," he sighed. "As I'm sure you've deduced by now, my control around you is always hanging by a thread. And you may not be susceptible to my charms, but you were still worried about me. The broth is a case in point."

"You've hidden your lack of control very well," she tried to keep the hurt at his avoidance from bleeding into her voice. "This time of year, most households always have broth warming and readily available. I was just ensuring that custom was adhered to."

"It's fine that you don't want to admit you were thinking about me. I know the truth," he smugly informed her. "And I grow weary of fighting it," he nudged her slightly to the right and sighed with visible satisfaction. "And now I have an excuse to abandon the struggle because we're standing beneath the mistletoe."

She glanced up. "I hate to correct you, but we're not. We're in the vicinity, and I'm not certain that warrants a kiss. I think tradition demands we stand directly beneath it. And I only see three berries. That means only three kisses. Are you sure you want to use one of them right now?"

"We'll agree to disagree. Before I let go of the desire I've been assuaging with my hand every single night since we argued, I need to know if we should be wary of an audience."

The thought of him stroking himself as he imagined her as part of a nightly ritual turned her veins to fire. "The girls are playing tiddly-winks in the sitting room."

He barked out a laugh. "Clem's been complaining she's too old for it since she turned ten."

"Ruby as well. The two of them looked like they'd rather walk across live coals when I asked them to set it up for the younger ones. They should be occupied for at least another thirty minutes."

"Perfect," he growled. "Then this needn't be a rushed affair with your skirts tossed over your head."

"In the middle of the afternoon?" she should be scandalized at the suggestion but knew the breathless excitement in her question wouldn't escape his notice.

"Yes, vixen. In the middle of the afternoon. Don't bother protest-ing, I heard the hitch in your breathing, and I know you're intrigued instead of scandalized. We're going to indulge our mutual fantasies in broad daylight. And I can take my time – maybe even enough time to demonstrate the use of my cravat."

"What makes you think I'd be amenable to such a demonstration? You can't prove it would be to my liking," she challenged.

He trailed a knuckle down her cheek, sliding it over the cut of her jaw and the defiant thrust of her chin. His rested his thumb be-neath the bow of her mouth, his hand wide enough that his fingers completely bracketed the left side of her throat, resting against her galloping pulse. He raised a brow, "I don't believe I need to prove how amenable you are. The pulse that feels like a runaway horse beneath my touch is all the proof I need."

"Maybe it's fear, not desire, which makes it thunder."

"Deceive yourself if you so choose. I'm finished trying to change your mind when you're set on a certain course. But I'm not the only one who will suffer because of your self-denial. You'll be inflicting harm on yourself as well," he exhaled gustily against her cheek. "Thoughts of you have occupied my thoughts, both awake and dreaming."

"I've been thinking about you as well. But I don't want those thoughts to consume me. This thing between us can't be more than an ephemeral liaison. We have less than four days until Silvester."

"If that's all the time you're willing to give me, I'll take it. Beginning right this moment."

The hand that had been resting against her pulse dropped to her waist. His other hand thudded into the wall on the other side. He pressed a kiss to her forehead and slid his grip to her thigh, squeezing and lifting the back of it until it was curled around his middle. "Up you go," he murmured into her hair.

She felt the sharp nip of his teeth on her earlobe, and the solid ridge of him against her. Her shoulders squared and she let her neck arch in invitation. Her skirts were draped around them, rising above the knee that clasped him to her bared mons. She'd never been so glad her stepson was too much of a skinflint to give her the funds for the purchase of the new joined pantaloons. Her threadbare split pair meant she could feel every inch of him encased in the dulled black broadcloth of his trousers as he slid along her crease.

He dropped his forehead, resting it against the shelf of hers. His gaze was fixed on the juncture of her thighs, and it heightened her arousal. A keening moan escaped her, and he moved his hand from the wall, covering her mouth. He didn't admonish her. He just shook his head. "No," he whispered. "We have to be quiet."

His admonition was tinder to a guttered spark inside her. The spark flared to life as his gaze bore into hers like the swift dart of a swallow from beneath the eaves, pinning her in place. The cloister of the house settled around them -devoid of any sound but the occasional creak of a board and the distant clang of pots and pans from the kitchen. She doubted their position would be revealed, and she decided railing against his stern demeanor meant he'd lift his hand from her mouth. She liked the feel of it there, the way his thumb brushed against her pulse in a steady rhythm. She set her teeth against his palm and his eyes darkened to reflections of the glossy green leaves of spurge laurel. The hardy bush grew wild on the edges of the moor, and the hard, nearly iridescent gleam of his irises was an echo of that wildness. It captivated her.

His lips hovered over her own. The top one was lush and full above the thin lower one marred by the cleft of the scar. She raised her hand and brushed her finger across its raised edges. He hissed, but not in pain. His leaf green eyes were full of surprise and arousal, like a cornered wolf that couldn't decide if it wanted to bite or nuzzle. A wolf locked in a battle between fight or flight because it couldn't decide if self-preservation or self-destruction was the wiser course of action.

The shoulders and back of his shirt were stiff with the dried evidence of his labor. The faint scent of horses clung to him, and the salty, heady aftertaste of his sweat. Like gritty iron sparks from an anvil she could taste on her tongue or the frothing head on a pint of richly brewed ale. She wanted to trace her fingers over every inch of his skin, to taste every single place perspiration had bathed his body. She wanted to push his braces down and wrench the edges of his shirt wide, pull it out of his waistband and send buttons clattering and scattering to dusty corners.

The pendulum of the clock across from them swung and clanged, marking the turn of the hour. Marking the handful of minutes that had passed since he anchored her to the wall. It felt like an hour, or a breath. It was a bright clarity that came from sifting through impulses and actions looking for a single constellation for guidance or navigation. And coming up empty-handed.

"The decision is yours," he reminded her.

She knew that surrendering to this madness, though the path of least resistance, was inherently perilous to her peace of mind. The walls around her heart were cracking like the greenware of unfired pottery in response to his presence. He snuck beneath them with the stealthy, quiet focus of a soldier sabotaging the cannons behind enemy lines. He muddled her brain and turned her muscles to pudding.

"Somehow your persistence has persuaded me," she conceded.

"You'll not regret it," he vowed. "But you were right to express trepidation at the precarious nature of our position. As much as I want to tup you here and now, we should decamp to the master suite."

She dropped her leg from around his waist, achingly aware of the slickness between her thighs and the way they would rub together as she climbed the stairs. She relished the way her body expressed its desire for him. Unapologetic and brazen despite her misgivings.

"You win for now, Thaddeus."

"It's not a war we're waging, Arie," he reproached as he clasped her hand. "I want to carry you the entire way, but I'm being cognizant of your delicate sensibilities. If we get caught and I cause you further embarrassment you may decide to abandon the idea altogether. And that would be a travesty. Because every inch of you deserves my reverence and adoration and I've been denied the indulgence far too long."

The house seemed miraculously empty. They didn't encounter a single intrepid soul as they wove their way to his door. He paused in front of it, laid his forehead against the gleaming oak surface and clenched the hand not holding hers at his side.

"What is it?" she prodded gently.

"I know we said this was a dalliance. But I have to tell you..." he gulped, unable to finish the sentence.

"I think I know," she rested her empty hand against his nape. "You've not had a woman in this bed with you since your wife died."

"When you say it aloud, it makes it so much more real. I've had female companionship since then, just not in this bed. Using this bed to satisfy my appetites seemed like a betrayal of her memory."

"I understand," she murmured. And she did. Even though her stomach curdled in disappointment, and she felt strangely bereft at the thought of leaving his side.

"Do you?" he whirled to face her, backing her against a wall once again. "I crave you, Arie. More than I ever craved her. Even though we were childhood sweethearts and she bore my children. It's the biggest betrayal of all because it makes me wonder if I settled for less. If I somehow missed the chance to befriend you the very first time I saw you and let things grow between us as we grew up."

"That wouldn't have worked out. You saw me for the first time at my wedding. And you were already married to someone else."

"The first time I saw you wasn't at your wedding."

"It wasn't?" His intensity puzzled her.

"No. The first time I saw you, you were sitting quietly in a chair holding your mother's hand."

"How is that possible?"

"Your father was desperate to save her and wanted the medical opinion of my father since he'd studied in London. I accompanied him because he needed my help at the farrier's."

"I remember, but I didn't notice you."

"The only thing I noticed about you was how quiet you were. You were sitting in that spindle-backed chair, one hand wrapped white-knuckled around your mother's, the other one white-knuckled and twisted in the fabric of your skirt. You just sat there, your world falling apart, the tears leaving tracks across the apples of your cheeks. I wanted to say something, but I knew whatever I said would sound trite. And I doubted you wanted a gangly, awkward sixteen-year-old boy expressing his sympathy."

"I would've looked askance and wouldn't have registered your words. Your assessment of the situation was correct," she took a deep breath. "My world was falling apart. I was almost thirteen, and I knew the burden of the household would fall on my shoulders soon. I knew I'd be responsible for raising my sisters because my father would be crippled by grief." She lightly stroked her fingers over his face. "We might've become friends, and we may not have. Everything happened as it was meant to happen."

He closed his eyes and let his hands fall from her hips. "You're right."

"The mood has slipped away from us, hasn't it?"

He shook his head. "I'm sorry. Would you be amenable to an hour or so of cuddling in front of the fire?"

"Yes. I'd be amenable to that. Especially if there's tea involved."

***

He'd dragged the quilt off the bed and wrapped it around them both. She was sitting between his raised knees, her back to his chest. His arms were loosely wrapped around her waist and his chin was resting on her shoulder. They were sharing her second cup of tea.

He'd grimaced at the first sip. "How can you drink that black swill?"

She'd laughed. "It's fortifying. And I think it tastes wonderful."

"It can still be fortifying with a touch of milk. Sweetening it isn't going to dilute the potency. I think someone dropped you on your head when you were a baby because you're addled if that's your preference," he sounded offended on behalf of tea drinkers everywhere.

"I think you're the one who was dropped on your head. Of course you'd prefer tea as thick and sickly sweet as treacle syrup."

"What do you mean by that?"

"I mean that your gruff demeanor doesn't fool me. I've seen you with your daughters and your heart is sheer mush. The preference for syrupy sweet tea is just the goodness you keep under lock and key leaking out."

"Humph," he grunted in response. But he didn't correct her. He tightened his arms around her waist instead and that was all the confirmation she needed.

The fire was lulling her to sleep. She finished her cup and set it on the floor beside them, letting her head drop back to his shoulder while they watched the violet and vermilion dance of the flames together.

SNOWFLAKES THAT STAY ON YOUR NOSE AND EYELASHES

When Arie woke up she was disoriented. The last thing she remembered was falling asleep in front of the fire. She was bundled in blankets and not a single shred of sunlight shown through the drapes. Someone was knocking on the door.

She blearily shoved to her feet and swung it open. Thaddeus was standing there. His greatcoat was buttoned all the way up his throat and a bright green knitted scarf that made his eyes flicker in the dim light of the candle he held was thrown over his shoulder. "Bundle up." He told her.

She gave him a quizzical look and shrugged her shoulders. "I expected you to demand I wear less clothing, not more. I confess I'm curious."

"You won't be sorry. I promise. Meet me downstairs as soon as you're able."

She donned her woolen gown and her flannel undergarments. She idly wondered if he was wearing a flannel waistcoat like Colonel Brandon's. He was a military man, so it was highly likely. The thought of seeing him in it made her brain turn to mush. All those long lines limned by firelight, with his strong feet bared and his hands fisted on his hips.

He looked up when she reached the landing, and watched her with an avid gaze the entire journey down the stairs. "I put on the clothes I wore here, because they're the warmest."

"I have a rug and a heated footrest to make you comfortable as well. Come." He extended his gloved hand toward her and she extracted one of hers from the muff to tangle their fingers together.

He tugged her through the silent house and out the side entrance, until they were standing in a pool of moonlight. Two chestnut geldings stamped their feet, the bells on their harness jingling at the movement. They were hitched to a sleigh.

The breath left her chest in an audible whoosh of air.

He slid a warming block under her feet, and shook out something that looked like a bearskin rug.

She wrinkled her nose. "Is that what I think it is? According to my sister Gertrude's penny dreadfuls about the Wild West, the coat of a bear is very pungent."

"You're correct, it's bearskin. From the bear that killed the wife and child of one of my best friends. It doesn't smell because he claims he scraped and conditioned it ad nauseam. He stalked and killed it for vengeance, but couldn't stand to have the reminder in his house. He gifted it to me the last time he visited from the wilds of America." He explained as he solicitously tucked it around her, even looping it over her head like a hood.

"It is very warm."

"It will keep the frostbite away. I wouldn't want this adorable snub of a nose to suffer." He kissed the dainty tip and then pulled a swath of fur over it so she was completely covered, with only her laughing eyes peeking up at him.

"What about you?" Her voice was muffled by the folds of bunting wrapped around her face.

"My team is fast. We're going to circle the farm pond and return to the barn to warm up." He pulled his muffler up over his nose and flicked the reins.

The team took off with a jaunt, and the bells he'd affixed to the harness pealed merrily across the yard.

Her yes sparkled as the sleigh swayed and swung over the snow, and he knew she was laughing, even though he couldn't hear or see it.

He smiled under the cover of his own scarf. He could finally see a glimmer of the girl who's joy had mesmerized him when she'd catapulted recklessly through the village streets. The weight of her arm against his and the warmth of her bundled thigh where it slid against his own as they jostled over a rut in the road made contentment unfurl in the pit of his stomach.

He cleared his throat and shifted on the seat, putting a sliver of space between them. "The horse trader brought the girls' pony today."

"Then it's fortuitous they've been cooped up inside. I'm sure they would have ruined the surprise." She paused as if weighing her words. "His delivery is confirmation that the roads aren't as treacherous as they were."

He knew what she was silently asking with her observation. "When I asked how perilous the journey was, he scoffed. He said rain and mud would never deter him from fulfilling a bargain. He took one of the green broke three-year-old fillies in exchange."

"So the roads are still difficult to navigate."

"According to him, yes."

"So the danger of intrusion is still improbable?"

He couldn't resist such an opening. "Intrusion from the outside world, yes. Intrusion in the bedchamber? Far from improbable. Imminent is a more apt characterization." He didn't dare glance her way as he made the pronouncement.

She sniffed, but he saw her lips twitch out of the corner of his eye, like she was holding back her mirth. "You're very sure of your charms."

"Mayhap you shouldn't have moaned so loudly when I was employing them."

"You weren't exactly quiet either."

"True. But I don't have a reputation for being quiet or pretending to be invisible. You have become adept at both. Until you threw me the key to unlocking everything you were afraid of revealing to the world."

He flicked the reins to speed up pace, and soon they were gliding over the packed snow like it was a sheet of glass beneath the horses' hooves.

Her laughter was a banner streaming all around them, and he thought she'd chosen to ignore his comment. He realized he was sorely mistaken when her hand crept from beneath the throw and landed on his thigh. The muscle grew tense beneath her touch when he realized she had no plans to move away or adjust her position.

"I should like to kiss you."

Surely he hadn't heard her correctly. They were in a sleigh and it was bloody cold. And if he was going to kiss her the way he wanted to kiss her, they needed to be somewhere it was safe to shed at least a few layers of clothing without getting frostbitten.

Maybe the wind was distorting her words.

"I didn't hear you."

She leaned closer, so close if they hit a rut in the road, she'd find herself with a face full of very aroused male when she tumbled into him. She didn't seem to care. She slid her grip further around his thigh and he could feel her breath caress the bare skin just below his ear. "I said I should like to kiss you."

So he hadn't been hallucinating.

He urged the horses toward the blackthorn thicket just over the rise on the other side of the road. They would be cold, but at least they'd be sheltered from the worst of the wind.

"Where are we going?" The lurch of the sleigh had thrown her back onto her side of the seat, so she was forced to practically shout her question.

"I'm getting my kiss."

As soon as they reached the thicket, he looped the reins around a trunk and lifted her down. He pressed her against the side of the sleigh and kissed the corner of her mouth that was quirked in a smile.

"That's your idea of a kiss?" She teased.

"Only the beginning of one."

Her lips were chilled against his own, and flitted over the evening stubble that dusted his cheeks and chin. "You should sport a full beard to keep you warm." She murmured.

"I was assured that ladies do not find beards attractive. That they think beards make men look like bears."

"I can assure you that is complete nonsense."

"So you wouldn't mistake me for a bear?"

She scoffed. "No. You're imposing enough to be a bear, but I'd liken you to a wolf instead."

"A wolf? Why is that?"

"The way you look at me sometimes, I feel like the girl from the story with the basket of goodies dangling from her wrist and the red cape shielding her from the elements."

"I make you feel like Little Red Riding Hood."

"Yes, that was the name of the story. A new version of it was recently released. My sister brought the collection home from the library and read it aloud to us when I visited them last month."

"I'll chase you through the woods any time you ask, Arie. But only if you stop talking now." He murmured as he nipped her earlobe.

"I can do that," she hastily agreed.

It was still bloody cold, and even though they were bundled against it, the layers of clothing weren't enough to bar the steady seep of winter damp. He pressed her more firmly into the side of the sleigh, so she was completely shielded from the flecks of ice swirling in the wind. She watched him as she slid off her mittens and pulled him toward her.

He captured her mouth again, warming it with the swipe of his tongue across her lush lower lip. He coaxed her to open to him and swept inside when she did. Their teeth clashed together and she slid her hands between the buttons of his coat, burrowing into his skin.

He set the edge of his teeth against the arch of her throat above the fur wrap, and bit the carotid pulsing under the chilled marble. He wanted to lay her back on the seat, drape the bearskin over their heads, feel the satin skin of her inner thighs, and dip his fingers into the wetness he knew he'd find there.

But he wasn't going to capitulate so easily. The wind was an icy dagger now, and he reluctantly drew away.

"We're going back to the house."

"It is very cold," she drowsily agreed.

"I have a delivery coming tomorrow and I have to rise very early. This kiss will have to be enough for tonight. For both of us."

"Then I'll be grateful we have three more nights after this one."

"We could have more, but you insist on being obstinate. I'm not going to stop trying to persuade you, but I'll give you a respite tonight."

When he lifted her back into the sleigh, he was even more solicitous than he'd been when they departed. And this time the weight of his arm was around her shoulder and she felt the comfort and safety of it through every layer she was bundled into.

When he dropped her hand from his at the door to her bedchamber and gave her a flitting peck of a kiss on the cheek before he made his way to his own bed, she rubbed her hand over her cheek for hours. She could still feel the ghost of his lips when she made her way down to breakfast the next morning.

Cream-Colored Ponies

"Girls, there's a surprise for you in the barn. Would you like to go see what it is?"

Claire's eyes rounded in wonder. "Only animals live in barns. And we all asked for a pony to share. Did you get us a pony, Papa?"

"You'll have to visit the barn."

All four of the younger girls sprang from their chairs, like dynamite was taped to their posteriors.

"Papa, we're not hungry." Rissa insisted.

"Yes, Papa. We're full."

"You've barely touched your breakfast and you'll be complaining this afternoon."

Claire approached him and flung her arms around his knees, nearly toppling him over. "Please, can we go now?"

Arie beamed at him from across the table. She held a napkin to her mouth, ineffectually suppressing her laughter. "I think you may as well abandon the kippers!" She finally chortled.

He sent her a look that conveyed the promise of punishment for her disrespect, but couldn't hold back his grin. He shrugged. "Girls, Arie seems to have the right of it. Perhaps we should abandon the kippers and go seek out your surprise."

Arie rose from her seat with a contained dignity that belied the sparkle in her eyes. It was full of mischief and he knew she was poking fun at him and expressing her affection. Ruby and Clem followed suit, emulating her more restrained demeanor. But their eyes were as full of excitement as the younger, more exuberant members of the party.

When he held his hand out, she slipped hers into it with no hesitation. Both Ruby and Clem focused on the contact, and exchanged a look loaded with speculation.

As they made their way to the barn, walking abreast on the shoveled path, Arie tilted her face upward. "This is all they'll want to talk about for days."

The girls were all in raptures over the pony and their enthusiastic plans dominated the entire day. She tried to teach them to knit and the twins insisted they wanted to learn to ride the pony bareback instead, and turn cartwheels on its back. When she asked where they would learn how to turn cartwheels on horseback, Rissa diffidently informed her they'd seen the traveling circus performers do it and they'd just run away and become a part of it.

More speculation about the pony was the only topic over dinner. She and Thaddeus had exchanged amused glances down the length of the table, punctuated by bursts of laughter. The entire scene had made her wistful.

When the children were finally nestled in their beds, she could do nothing but toss and turn. The sheets felt like they were abrading her skin, and she couldn't find a comfortable spot. After the intense conversation the evening before, she was betting she wouldn't be spending the night alone. But the moon was high and she was still alone.

Her musings were interrupted by a gentle rap on the door. She didn't need to peer through the keyhole to identify the interloper.

She pulled the door open and leaned against it. Blocking his entry. He raised a brow at her obstruction.

"You weren't expecting me."

"I'd almost given up. After accusing me of obstinacy last night and the awkwardness between us about using your bedchamber, I wasn't going to presume." She determinedly tightened the tie closing her wrapper.

"Even after I made it clear during our sleighride that I had designs on you?"

"You didn't make it that clear," she insisted. "You just said you weren't going to give up on persuading me."

"My apologies. I thought I was being very clear about my intentions," he bowed at the waist. "Allow me to clear things up so there can be no mistake."

"Go ahead," she urged.

"I've brought this," he stretched a white cravat between his fists, and snapped it in the air.

"What if I've changed my mind and I don't feel like being trussed up for your delectation?"

"Then I'll allow you to truss me up again," he rumbled.

The memory of him straining against the drapery bindings made her blood heat. She swiped her tongue across suddenly dry lips.

"You still haven't shaved," she inanely remarked.

"I grew accustomed to my beard during the war. For the first time, soldiers were permitted to have them. It's quite useful at keeping the wind from chapping your face. Especially during weather like this," he shrugged. "Besides, if your reaction to the rasp of my whiskers between your legs is any indication, you have no complaints."

She wanted to refute his devilish observation, but he was only speaking the truth. *She had liked the rasp of his beard against her inner thighs.* "I suppose there's no point in making you linger in the hallway," she grabbed his arm above the elbow and tugged him forward. He kicked the door shut and lifted her against him, pushing her wrapper from her shoulders.

"Legs around my waist like a good girl," he demanded as his palms enveloped the cheeks of her ass in a firm grip and her robe fluttered to the floor like a white flag of surrender.

"I don't like being a good girl. I'd think you'd know that by now," she countered.

He growled into her mouth as he bit her bottom lip. "That's why I brought the cravat."

"I still haven't agreed to that plan."

"You will," he confidently replied, his gaze a smoldering velvet green.

He licked the indentation his teeth had left and raised one of his hands from her waist, bracketing her chin to hold her steady. "Open," he commanded.

The cold austerity in his tone made her stomach clench. It also had the opposite effect. It made her want to simultaneously deny him and strangle him. She'd been honest when she said she didn't want to subject herself to his cruel little mercies. When he swirled his tongue into her mouth, she bit it.

"Bollocks!" he reared his head back. "Your fangs are a weapon," he tightened his grip on her waist, his fingers curling into her skin. "That hurt."

"Good," she murmured. "I don't appreciate being told what to do."

"You're playing with fire, vixen," he grumbled.

"Maybe I'd be more pliable if you asked me nicely."

"You don't fool me. You're not refusing because I didn't ask. You're refusing because you're not the one in control. You manipulated nearly every detail of our last encounter and you don't like feeling powerless."

This is why he was like a stick of dynamite to her equilibrium. He saw her too clearly. She wanted to shrink away from his scrutiny. And bask in the fact that he paid such scrupulous attention to her. "Fine," she sighed. "I won't bite your tongue again."

He grinned. "But you'll bite me elsewhere? Anyone else would've said they wouldn't bite me again, period. But you were very specific."

She couldn't quell her answering grin. "I was very purposefully specific."

"I might not complain," he ruefully admitted. "Are you comfortable taking our discussion to the bed?"

"What's wrong with the wall?"

His eyes swept over her body, lingering on her peaked nipples. She wanted to arch her back and inch closer to his insidious heat. "The wall makes it difficult to use the cravat," he clarified.

"You seem to have changed your mind rather quickly about pursuing this," she motioned between them. She wasn't going to let him blow hot and cold, like a will o' wisp fluttering in the breeze. "If we're doing this, then we're doing it. You need to abandon any notions of guilt you're harboring, or it won't work."

"I'm chipping away at my guilt. I'll have no regrets about laying you down on the bed behind us."

"Then what are you waiting for?"

"I'm assuming that means I have your permission, since you haven't explicitly given it."

"Yes, you nodcock. You have my permission to ravage me."

He strode towards the bed while she clung to him like a limpet hanging onto a rock. He tossed her onto it and pinned her beneath him before she could scramble away. "Arms stretched over your head."

She did as he asked. Not because she liked obeying him, but because she was intrigued by the thought of what came next. He yanked the cravat from his front pocket with a flourish and leaned forward on his knees so he could reach the headboard. The posts and railing were made of solid brass, and he kept his eyes on her and his hands as he tied. And tied. And tied.

"Nothing to secure my ankles?" she asked, only half-jesting. She tugged experimentally on his handiwork. To no avail.

"I'll use drapery cords to tether you there."

She couldn't hold back the shiver. She would be well and truly trussed up. "I feel like a vestal virgin about to service an emperor."

"I want to erase the memory of your husband's touch on your body."

"That will require little effort on your part," she scoffed. "I don't think he ever touched anything besides my arse. And that was rarely. And never pleasant," she grimaced.

"Then my task will be all the more rewarding," he murmured. He stood up. "No wriggling while I get the cords."

Wriggling was unlikely. She was firmly locked in place by knots that felt like they were made on the devil's playground. Faster than she could've imagined, he was standing at the foot of the bed, gazing down at her. The cords dangled between his fingers.

"You're being terribly slow and melodramatic," she playfully chided.

"Before I use these, there's something else I need to do."

He climbed onto the bed and leaned over just far enough to set his hands on the frayed edge of her collar. He growled. Then he smirked.

Her breath caught in her throat.

Then he tore the gown straight down the middle with one greedy swipe.

"Ruining my borrowed clothes was the something you needed to do?" She asked with a smirk of her own.

"Yes. I wanted to rip your shapeless nightmare in half when we met in the barn. And this repellent monstrosity isn't much of an improvement. You may as well be wearing a funeral shroud."

"Now I have nothing to keep me warm."

"You have me," he replied, and tapped his chest to emphasize his point.

"That's not entirely true. I have you for less than a week, and…" he placed his hand over her mouth, just as he had in the hallway.

She glared at him.

"No," he corrected with a firm shake of his head. "You're not allowed to cloud our time here with thoughts of the future. Not tonight."

"Then start distracting me," she demanded.

He leaned back on his haunches, the steely determination of his gaze trailing over every bared inch of her skin. A single finger arrowed toward her, and she inhaled with anticipation. He lightly grazed one taut, furled nipple, and then the other one, with his knuckles and she couldn't shove down the moan that clogged her throat. His knees bracketed the length of her hips and upper thighs, and he wrapped his arms around the bed spindles. He lowered his body, tantalizing her with the scrape of his hair-roughened chest against the tips of her breasts. She thrashed uselessly beneath him, wanting to prolong that delicious contact, but held captive by her bindings.

"At least I haven't blindfolded you as you did me."

"I don't know that I would have complained," she hoarsely admitted.

"Next time."

"You're confident there will be a next time?"

"Yes, we have at least four more days to explore each other. And I intend to make full use of them."

He lowered his head to her breast, swirling his tongue down the valley of her cleavage, letting his hot breath and silken mouth brush against the edge of her curves. "You're a demon," she muttered when he skated around the goosebumps surrounding the part of her she wanted him to envelop.

He dropped his hands from the headboard and cupped her cheeks. His lips caressed hers with intentional languor. As if they had all the moments in the world at their disposal, cocooned in a shroud of golden hours that kept the world from intruding. He nipped the outline of her lips, and then sucked her tongue into the depths of his mouth. He stroked and tangled, mimicking the capricious, feinting dance of a fencing master and a student. When he finally ended the kiss they were both breathing heavily, like they'd both just lifted a carriage from the mud. Her chest felt crushed, not because of his weight, but because of the weight of her feelings. He lowered his forehead to hers, and then dropped lower on her torso, bracing himself over her once again.

His arms were nearly straight, slightly bent at the elbows, when he finally, finally...

The suction of his mouth was hot and dark and sweet. Like being caught in the eye of a storm, blinded by the dust and debris, waiting for the bolt of lightning you dreaded but knew would at least light your path. She wanted to tunnel her hands through the salt and pepper strands of his hair, rake it back from his forehead and smooth it behind his ears. Just as she would handle anything she deemed precious.

The thought of seeing him across a crowded assembly room, and not having the freedom to do those things, of being unable to indulge in that tender familiarity, cracked her heart wide open. She squeezed her eyes shut and concentrated on the way he felt. Memorizing it so she could hoard every second like a glittering gem against the inevitable separation.

He lifted his head far too soon. "You've gone quiet, love."

She wanted to push back the rebellious lock of hair that always seemed to be falling in his eyes. "Just enjoying the way you feel," she forced a smile.

"You've gone quiet for another reason."

"You forbade me from dwelling on it, so I'm trying not to."

His eyes softened. "I'm doing the same. I need to focus on torturing you rather than cherishing you."

He bent over her again, clamping one of his hands at her waist like a vise. His wicked, talented, mouth that should be banned from existence on all seven continents, lowered to her chest once again. His tongue lashed across the swollen tips of her breasts, and his fingers stroked her wetness through her folds. He rubbed his knuckle over her clitoris and groaned against her, the rumble of his voice making her throb and clench around his hold.

She bucked beneath him, desperate to drive them closer. He pushed her back to the mattress, sliding his hand down her thigh and wrapping it tightly to hold her still.

"Are you ready for me?" His voice rumbled against her again, the gravel and grit a strumming invitation.

"Yes," she pleaded. She wanted to feel tethered to him. She wanted to grip the hard length of his cock as it pressed deep inside her.

His eyes glittering, he rested over her in a kneeling position, his knees cupping her lower hips. He threw his head back and thrust inside her. He balanced himself on solid thighs and corded forearms, leaning away, his eyes fixed on the place they were joined. "You're so fucking wet for me," he groaned, his eyes gleaming with possession.

She couldn't bring herself to blush. Knowing her arousal was tinder to his own, that the clench of her body around his cock made his cheeks flush and his body tighten in concentration, was a heady aphrodisiac.

"How does it feel to be stuffed full of my cock? Is the slide of my head against your pretty little clit making you see stars?"

His filthy praise did make her see stars. Shooting stars that cascaded from her tightly closed lids to the spot he was ferociously swiveling his hips against. "I see stars," she gasped.

"Good, before this night is over I'm going to make sure you see the whole fucking galaxy."

She cried out, her body tensing beneath his when he buried himself to the hilt, holding himself suspended against her so he could grind against her throbbing clitoris. She saw the whole fucking galaxy. She saw the entire fucking universe. She reveled in using the filthy descriptor – even if it was only in her head.

"Arie," he groaned, her name a litany on his lips. He pulled himself outside the lock and key of her body, thrust in again, jerked three times and filled her with his seed.

The hunger that had flared between them was only temporarily abated, but the muscles in Arie's legs and arms were burning. "Will you untie me, now?"

"Of course, vixen." He knelt down to unbind her ankles and massaged the marks the cords had left on her skin. Then he reached above her head and untied his cravat from her wrists. He brought each one to his mouth, soothing the red marks with the cool caress of his lips.

Her eyes blurred with tears. Both at his gentle touch and the fact he'd spilt his seed inside her. She'd wanted him to fill her in every way. "Thank you for giving me this. Twice now," she mumbled through the sob lodged in her throat like a boulder. "I wanted you to fill me. So I'd be filled with something."

Thaddeus cupped her cheek in his hand. "Arie. There's no guarantee you're infertile. Your husband was an octogenarian when he took you to his bed. As I told you earlier, there's every chance the fault was his, not yours."

"But he has children," she reminded him.

He smiled at her naivete. "Yes, he has children. And they are of an age with you. He was a man of much more vigor when he fathered them. As I told you before - if there are consequences to our joining I will take care of you and I'll brook no argument."

"So you're trying to protect me again," the thought of him sparing her future difficulty or embarrassment infuriated her for some reason. Irrationally, she wanted to thrust him off her and pommel him with her fists.

"I'll always do everything I can to protect you," he brushed a curl from her temple, just as she'd longed to do to him. "Even if this is one of the last times I can acknowledge what we've shared or touch you again."

The thought of him never touching her again hollowed out her insides. "You can at least ask me to dance at the next village assembly."

"I cannot. I should seek a wife to be a mother to my daughters, and you've already told me you're not interested in the position. For secretive reasons you're unwilling to share. And if I look forward to touching you, even when it's in the middle of something as innocuous as a country reel, I won't look at other women."

"Why wouldn't you look at other women?" She prodded, holding her breath in anticipation of his answer.

"You know why." She could easily stumble into the lush, glimmering depths of his eyes. And lose her way trying to navigate away from their murky jade spell.

She did know why. She sighed. And then sighed again. Wishing they were anyone other than who they were. That she was Emma and he was Knightley. Independently wealthy and free to love where she chose.

He stood up and went to the washstand on the other side of the room. He returned with a damp piece of linen and meticulously wiped away the evidence of their union.

***

The children came bursting through the bedroom door at the crack of dawn.

"We think Santa Claus was here last night!" shouted Callie.

Thaddeus sat up, the sheets pooling around his waist while she burrowed down further and clutched them to her chest. She wanted to pull them over her head and hide, but it was too late. Rissa had spotted her.

"Good morning, Arie," she beamed. "Why is our papa in your bed? Were you giving him a back rub? Sometimes Callie and I do that after he's been working on the fences all day or when the ewes are lambing."

Arie seized on the explanation with relief. "Yes! I was giving your papa a back rub." She could feel Thaddeus shaking beside her, trying to hold in his laughter. "Why don't you girls meet us in the parlor? We'll be down in a quarter of an hour."

As soon as she heard them clattering down the stairs she turned around to glare at him. She balled her fist and punched him in the arm with all her might.

He burst out laughing. "You're a wee devil, just like them. Why so angry?"

"We should've been more careful! Why did we fall asleep so quickly?"

"Do you really need me to answer that question?"

"No, it was rhetorical. We should get dressed before they decide we're taking too long."

"You know they've likely dumped the contents of their stockings on the floor already?"

"Of course they have," she grinned. "I'd expect nothing less."

"Then there's truly no reason to rush. You look very delectable half-dressed," he leered up at her.

"You're incorrigible. And every exhibition of your skills so far has lasted at least an hour."

"I've heard no complaints."

"And you won't. But right now we can't afford an hour-long demonstration."

"You're a termagant. Intent on depriving me of sleep and pleasure."

"I've never noticed you sleeping past dawn," she pointed out.

"That's irrelevant," he groused.

"No, it's not. It just proves you're being difficult," she finished buttoning her shirtwaist. "I'm off to the kitchens for some tea. I'll meet you in the parlor."

"No morning kisses?"

"If I come over there and kiss you, you're going to drag me back into the bed."

"Fine," he teased. "I'll see you downstairs."

Just as they'd dominated the dinner conversation with talk of their ponies, the children dominated the Christmas feast. They were meticulously going through the contents of their stockings, bartering for the things they wanted more of. Callie favored butterscotch candies, and Rissa favored peppermint. Ruby wanted all of the ribbons and Pearl wanted everyone's pencils.

When Arie asked her why, she was surprised by the answer delivered in typical Pearl fashion. "How else am I to record my scientific observations?"

"What kinds of observations?" asked Thaddeus.

Pearl smiled. "Like why Ruby claims to have such delicate sensibilities yet can't seem to keep the goose grease from dripping down her chin."

Pearl had nearly leapt from her chair after that pronouncement. Obviously a victim of Ruby's errant boot to her shin. "You're not supposed to comment on things like that," she glared at her sister.

"Young ladies, I think it's time for some music in the parlor," Thaddeus interrupted, trying to diffuse the impending squabble. "Ruby, will you do the honors of accompanying us on the pianoforte?"

Ruby blushed at the compliment. She was becoming very accomplished and was eager to show off her newly acquired expertise at any opportunity. "I only know the waltz."

Thaddeus's eyes caught and held Arie's. "That's perfect," he murmured.

He proffered his elbow to escort her into the garlanded parlor. Every nook and cranny was ablaze with a lighted candle, and the tree watched over them from the corner of the room – like a steadfast toy soldier.

Ruby settled herself on the bench, her fingers gracefully poised over the ivory keys.

"Wait, Ruby!" Rissa called out. "They have to bow and curtsey first."

"So we do, poppet," Thaddeus agreed. "Thank you for reminding us."

They exchanged courtesies, both bending low to the floor. Humbling themselves to each other in this one small way.

When the first note emerged from the pianoforte, both tinny and robust, and the music swelled into every festooned corner of the room, Arie lost herself to its joyous cadence. Thaddeus swept her back and forth, his arm tighter about her waist than would've been acceptable in polite company. With every step, his legs brushed against her own beneath the fall of her skirts, his foot sliding innocuously between her slippers like a covert invitation.

When the music rose to a crescendo, he spun her into a dizzying pirouette before he dipped her low over the back of his arm. The tendrils of hair that had escaped from her ruthlessly pinned braids dangled over the floor as he bent her over. His eyes fastened on the supple, suspended curve of her body and swept over her parted lips. He swiped his tongue across his own, like he was tempted beyond bearing.

He was closing the distance between them when they simultaneously realized the music had stopped. Their gazes clashed, neither one inclined to glance in another direction. She was still hovering over the floor, braced over his arm, poised like a bird caught midflight.

He raised her to her feet once again, bracing his forearm across her midriff. She stumbled, still wrapped in the feel of his hands and eyes on her. She placed her palms on the solid wall of his chest to catch her breath and regain her equilibrium.

The children were watching them with wide eyes. Ruby's hands had fallen away from the pianoforte and were now clasped beneath her chin. Her eyes were locked on them with a rapturous gaze full of rainbows and happy endings.

Thaddeus assisted Arie to her feet, clearing his throat. He turned to Ruby as if they hadn't just been mesmerized by each other. To the exclusion of their surroundings and everything else that existed outside the bubble between them. "Thank you, Ruby," he bowed toward the beaming girl. "You are quite skilled and do your tutors credit."

"I loved watching the pair of you," she confessed, eyes shining.

This observation prompted another throat clearing. "Perhaps you'll have another opportunity to demonstrate your mastery at the next village assembly."

"I'd love that!" she intoned.

He turned his attention to Arie again, bowing over her hand. He lifted it to his mouth and grazed the pulse fluttering in her wrist. "Thank you, ma'am for a lovely sojourn across the dancefloor."

"You're welcome," she replied. And wondered if this was the end. Would he knock on her door tonight? Or was this waltz his way of saying goodbye?

"Rissa and Callie, will you make sure Ruby and Pearl have everything they need for their return to their home? Arie and I have much we need to discuss."

The girls gave them good night hugs and scampered towards their bedchamber.

When they'd gone, he slipped her hand into the crook of his elbow and strode in the direction of his study.

He leaned against the wide oak desk and crossed his arms over his chest. "What are we going to do, Arie?" he asked in exasperation.

"What do you mean? We shall go on as before. Two ships in the night and all that," she waved dismissively.

"You know that's impossible," he growled. "I haven't felt this alive since I left for war six and a half years ago. You awaken something in me I thought long dormant. And I refuse to set it aside because it's inconvenient or inappropriate," he fiercely elaborated.

"I've already told you that I need to honor the agreement I made with Hugh," she stiffly replied.

"But you haven't told me why," he barked. "And I deserve to know why, Arie."

She took a deep breath. It wasn't that she was ashamed or embarrassed of the decisions she'd made. They just seemed suddenly petty and mercurial in the shadow of what lay between them. "I already told you I received nothing when my husband died," he shook his head, encouraging her to go on. "I was utterly devastated. You know that marriage was the death of all my dreams. I almost had a nest egg from training the dogs, but I had to give it to my sisters. The only reason I kept a kernel of hope was because my husband agreed to a marriage settlement of fifty pounds for each of them instead of a widow's portion. Because he knew that Sadie's prize money and what he could demand for her litters far exceeded that. But that promise wasn't incorporated into the will."

Thaddeus shook his head. "I can finish the story. You confronted Hugh, probably distraught, and he agreed to help you."

"Yes."

"But his acquiescence didn't come without strings. He's a born manipulator, so I'm sure he designed the bargain to no one's advantage but his own."

"I was grateful he was so accommodating."

Thaddeus stepped forward. "But he wasn't accommodating, Arie. He was opportunistic."

"What do you mean?"

"Did you know that he sold two pups from Sadie's last litter to the Queen's Royal Shepherd at Balmoral?"

She was abashed that she hadn't known that. "No, I didn't know that," she acknowledged.

"Each of those pups commanded three hundred pounds apiece."

Her eyes widened. "That's far and above the cost of the marriage settlement for my sisters."

"Exactly. What you asked for is a mere pittance in comparison," he ran an angry hand through his hair, dislodging his queue and disheveling it so the errant lock dipped over his forehead, obscuring his eyes. "He purposefully took advantage of you because he's a cheapskate and an arse."

"What should I do? I can't just leave. What about the girls? Their mother is terrible, you know that," she wrung her hands in front of her. "And if I leave, my sisters won't have the choices they deserve."

He strode forward and grabbed her twisting hands. "Please think about marrying me, Arie. That's what you can do. Think about a future here with me. Helping me raise my daughters and making my house a home with your warmth and sass and light. Talk to your sisters. Think about it as long as you need to."

"That may be quite a while."

"I'll wait for you. There's no one else for me and if I can't have you by my side, no one else will suffice. I refuse to pressure you into anything because you've been manipulated and mauled your entire life. I want you to choose me, to choose us, because it makes you happy. For no other reason."

"I'm still leaving tomorrow."

"I know. And I think you need to. You need some distance so you can see your path with more clarity of purpose. I'm not going anywhere," he lifted her chin and pressed a soft kiss on her nose. "Will you lie in my arms tonight?"

"I will," lying in his arms might not give her clarity, but it would give her comfort.

***

She woke to the pale light of dawn and couldn't stretch because his arm was wedged around her waist and a very muscular leg liberally covered in dark hair trapped her own against the mattress. She squirmed to loosen his hold. "No," he murmured into the shell of her ear. She could feel his hardness nestled at her back. A poignant reminder that their interlude was nearing its end. The repaired carriage would retrieve them in mere hours.

"I have to make sure Ruby and Pearl are respectably attired and scrubbed clean," she protested.

"I want to hold you for a while longer."

"I want you to hold me, but duty calls. Quite loudly and insistently." She carefully extricated herself from their pile of tangled limbs and moved toward the washstand. The water in the ewer was cold but bracing. She dipped the linen cloth in it and swiped her face, her armpits and the tenderness between her legs. She'd be sore from the remnants of their vigorous night, but she had no regrets. She'd spent her last night of freedom exactly as she'd wished. She didn't want it to end quite yet. She climbed into their bower and snuggled up to the human furnace at her back. His arm pulled her closer and she felt his cheek against the crown of her head. His thumb slowly stroked over her navel and she wanted to arch into his touch. Just one more time.

Somewhere In My Youth or Childhood

The meager light of the winter morning spilled across the bed, gilding the cheekbones of the woman curled against him. Thaddeus wanted to keep the world at bay. He wanted to hold her in his arms and forget about mucking out stalls and fixing doll heads and trying to learn to resew a button. He was losing her because she didn't think this life he'd offered her was enough. Because she was determined to keep sacrificing her future happiness for the sake of others. He was determined to speak with her sisters. If they were aware of the concessions she was making for them, of everything she was surrendering without fighting, they would intervene. From what Thad had observed, they were all productive members of village society with their own roles and aspirations. They kept a cozy, welcoming home and he was mystified about Arie's motivations. Did she still think of her very capable, competent sisters as the little girls she'd had to raise? If she did, they all needed to jolt her out of her misconceptions.

He'd unequivocally let her know what he wanted. And she wouldn't let herself admit it's what she wanted too. Even though he understood her refusal, he didn't accept it and it hurt deeply. More than the knife that had slashed his face in the heat of battle. More than the touch of embers that left their marks on his skin. He felt her impending loss almost as keenly as the loss of his wife and sons. Because he was going to be forced to watch her leave. To watch her choose something other than a future with him.

"Will you be accompanying Ruby and Pearl when they return for their riding lessons?"

"You know that's unwise." She mumbled into her pillow.

"Why is it unwise, Arie? Was this just an interlude you'll fondly remember while you're instructing the housemaids on how to properly dust mantels or polish the silver?"

"You know it was more than that."

"I'm not sure I do. I've made it very clear how I feel and what I want."

She rolled to face him. "You haven't said the words. I know that doesn't diminish the intensity of your feelings, and saying the words aloud isn't going to change my mind. You said you choose me and you'll wait for me, but there are declarations you still haven't made."

"Then there's no point in me saying them. I've told you my loyalty is yours. You brought light into our house and lives that I was unaware had disappeared. I told you I will wait. Because I will. Because no other woman will fit into the space you created here. But I won't say those three words until I know I'm saying them to seal our forever. Because I know you won't take the risk of saying them in return."

"At least you acknowledge it's a risk for me."

"You've only shared some of what you've gone through. I know you're sad, Arie. I want to believe you weren't sad here. I want you to know that if you choose me, if you choose us, I'll do everything in my power to ensure you're never sad or lonely again. I know you're afraid to let go because you're so accustomed to guarding everything you are and keeping others out with a smile that's not real. They don't know you as I've come to know you."

"You don't know me as well as you think you do. I'm a coward, Thaddeus."

He cupped her cheek in his palm and brushed a kiss over her forehead. "You're not a coward, Arie. You're the bravest, strongest woman I've ever met. This isn't about cowardice. It's about your reluctance to believe in yourself and claim the happiness you deserve."

"You've been on the battlefield. It is cowardice." She insisted.

"That's the point I'm trying to make, Arie. I've led men into battle. I've seen true cowardice and bewilderment reflected in the faces of my commanding officers and some men who were under my charge. I repeat -you are not a coward."

"Then why am I so afraid of what my life will look like tomorrow?" She murmured.

"Because you know how petty and vindictive your stepson can be. Because you know that the rumors are making their rounds through the village and you may be facing slander and shaming when you take your seat in the family pew come Sunday morning."

"You don't think our sojourn here has escaped everyone's notice?"

He snorted. "Nay, Vixen. I don't. If my mother was concerned enough to send me a message when the roads were still hazardous, we haven't escaped notice. There will be repercussions. And I'm telling you that you needn't face them alone."

"What more can be done to me that life hasn't already seen fit to bombard me with?" She bitterly replied.

"That's why you deserve peace and happiness. And you're too bloody stubborn to claim them and take what I'm offering you."

"I appreciate what you're offering me. But I can't take it. Can we please stop discussing it and enjoy the few moments that remain?"

"You know I'm not giving up that easily. I'll accost you after church if I need to. I won't let him win."

"My choice isn't my stepson winning. It's me winning by making my sisters' lives better."

"This isn't the end of this discussion, but I'm going to respect your wishes for the present." He kissed her cheek and eased up so he could leverage himself out of the bed.

He wanted to grit his teeth when his feet landed on the cold floor. Like the conscientious father he strove to be, he'd used all the rugs in the girls' room. The brittle air seeped through his thick wool socks and he almost stumbled from the shock of it against his soles.

"Bloody hell, the floor is frigid."

She snuggled under the cover and looked up at him with eyes full of laughter. "I want to sympathize with you. But you expression..."

He swooped down and scooped her up, tossing her over his shoulder. "How should I punish you for your impertinence?" He slid his hand over the curve of her rump bundled beneath the sheets. "I don't know if I should place you over my knee or just let you experience the agony of this damn floor yourself."

"I vote for being placed over your knee," she smokily whispered.

"That would distract me from all the things I need to do this morning. If I do that, it'll be hours before we leave this room. And we don't have hours."

He swung her to the floor and she yelped in dismay when her feet landed on the bare boards. She shuddered, and stepped onto his feet, wrapping her arms around his waist like he was about to give her dancing lessons. "You weren't exaggerating." She huddled into him.

He chuckled into the tousled mess of her hair. "I always tell the truth. I should be punishing you, but I'm going make your tea and let you snuggle under the blankets instead." He placed her on the bed and wrapped the coverlet more snugly around her. "I'll be back soon."

She watched him go and wanted to thump her chest to make the hollow feeling disappear. Their time together, this indulgence and freedom to run away and ignore the consequences of her actions was coming to an end. She'd soon be forced to face cold floorboards alone, to make her own morning tea and bow her head to the task of passively accepting whatever vitriol Hugh and Violet hurled in her direction.

The Clock in the Hallway is Sadly Clanging

Her stepson's coach barreled up to the house. The coachman sawed on the reins and struggled to bring the team to a halt.

Arie stood in the drive, her arms crossed over her chest. She relished the impending confrontation. Thaddeus stood protectively behind her, the solid warmth of his palm searing the small of her back through his glove.

Hugh tumbled from the carriage before it came to a complete stop. He paced angrily toward them, as if Cerberus nipped at his heels.

His expression was furiously tight and he pointedly glared at Thaddeus's arm looped around her waist. "I am not pleased," he intoned.

"You're never pleased," she muttered.

"You've made fools of Violet and me. Your sojourn on this farm with no chaperone, and no other guests besides our children, did not go unnoticed."

"You condoned this trip the morning we left and I can't believe the antics of a widow who is firmly on the shelf would be enough gossip to feed the gristmill. "

"Your lascivious behavior is all the more egregious because you're incapable of understanding its repercussions," he pompously lectured.

"See here, there's no reason to insult her." Thaddeus interjected.

Hugh rounded on him. "There's every reason. I can understand your lack of decorum. You still wear a queue and a cravat for god's sake. But not her. You've succeeded in morally bankrupting her and adversely impacting the future of my children."

Thaddeus scoffed and took a step forward, his fists curled at his waist. "That's utter shite. She's a grown woman capable of making her own independent decisions. The fallout from those decisions falls on our shoulders alone, not those of the children."

"She's meant to set an example for my daughters. An example of a woman conscious of her place. She did exactly the opposite. Instead, she's been cavorting around like your whore," he spat.

The expression on her lover's face hardened. He surged forward, his fist colliding with her stepson's chin. Hugh went spinning to the ground, clasping his face. "I'll see you in court for assault," he sputtered.

"I'd like to see you try. You're not well liked here. Especially not by the village merchants. You have a horrible habit of letting your bills lapse and castigating those who don't deserve it."

"I know you rogered her," he hissed in return. "And the whole village knows the two of you were stranded here together for the entirety of the snowstorm."

"That's not a threat considering what was happening at the manor. Do they also know about the shenanigans that happened there? I heard there were orgies."

"There weren't any orgies!" he whined. "Much to the disappointment of the more licentious guests. But there was little I could do to stop their nightly games of musical doors."

"That behavior is much more scandalous than a widow and a widower engaging in mutual comfort."

"But none of those people are in charge of instructing my daughters. You both acted with inadequate decorum. If she doesn't want to pack her meager belongings when we return and be cast out upon her ear, she'll avoid you." He ran a wild hand through his hair. "If she avoids you, the gossip will fade."

"I don't want to avoid him or his daughters." Arie countered. "And I'm standing right in front of you. Stop speaking as if I weren't. I don't give a fig about my reputation. I deserve to make decisions about my own future and who it includes."

Hugh narrowed his gaze on her. "If he didn't offer you marriage, you don't have much of a choice. And neither do your sisters if I withhold the dowry I promised."

"You have no grounds to do so. I'm entitled to receive some sort of compensation for the last twelve years I've spent laboring in your household."

"I can and I would. That promise was made in exchange for your care of my daughters. I don't care about the indulgence you think you extracted from my father. He was obviously placating you as there was no reference or inclusion of your alleged agreement in the will. Your licentious behavior demonstrates you're unfit to serve as governess to my daughters. I'm willing to give you another chance because I won't have your starvation on my conscience," he informed her in his typically patronizing tone.

"I don't ask for a salary, and I've been at your beck and call the last two years. The least you can do is honor the promise you made me, regardless of whether it was part of your father's will and despite any attachment I may have to Mr. St. Simon." Thaddeus had been right when he'd described Hugh as opportunistic. Hugh was manipulating her to achieve his own ends. She doubted he ever intended to fulfill his part of the bargain.

"I'm under no obligation to honor that promise, and well you know it. Because you had no bequests from my father's estate, I suffer your presence and upkeep as an act of mercy. You enjoy the food and shelter provided at the manor solely due to my beneficence. You'd do well to remember that."

"Ah, yes. There it is," she retorted caustically. "Let's make certain the woman who did nothing but succor your father in his dotage is the one to be reviled. Let's make certain the woman is made to suffer for finding herself in a situation not of her own making."

"Your suffragette sympathies will not serve you well. Women are inherently weaker of mind. It is a proven fact. You should be grateful for my leniency in this matter."

"Come now, man." Thaddeus remonstrated. "You can't truly believe that tripe?"

"It's not tripe!" sputtered Hugh. "As I said, it's been scientifically proven. My stepmother, like all women, is prone to hysteria and can't be trusted to make these decisions for herself. It is my responsibility as an upstanding citizen of the parish to guard her virtue."

Thaddeus looked like he was about to launch another punch. She laid her hand on his arm. "It's fine," she told him. "This is exactly what we knew would happen before we even set foot on this path. I am perfectly capable of dealing with the fallout and making the sacrifices I need to make. Because now I'll have the memory of you." She rose to her toes and bussed his cheek.

Thaddeus wanted to arrest that kiss, to turn his head just enough to catch her lips with his own. He wanted to sweep her into his arms or throw her over his shoulder and carry her back into his house and into his life. He wanted to tie her up with every cravat he could find and never let her out of his sight.

He watched as the coachman assisted her into the carriage. He watched as she left with a flutter of her hand and a grimace he supposed was meant to be a smile but conveyed nothing but their shared misery. He stood helplessly in the drive, his hands clenched so hard they ached.

***

Ten days later, Thaddeus deposited his daughters with their grandmother and knocked on the door of the cottage at the end of the coaching road.

There was a muffled curse from inside the bowels of the dwelling and the entry swung open. The dark-haired woman fisted one hand on her hips and brandished a broom in his direction.

"I'm here..."

"That's enough from you. I know who you are and why you're here. You broke my oldest sister's heart, Thaddeus St. Simon."

"I think she broke mine too." He somberly confessed.

Her scrutiny at his confession made him feel like he was facing the Spanish Inquisition. "Well you certainly haven't tried to make amends."

"There were things I needed to get in order. I could use an ally."

"And you think I'm a good candidate for this alliance?"

"I don't know. I think you want your sister to be happy and I think you know that's something I can give her."

"I don't know that. So far you've only made her miserable."

"I just want the chance to discuss something with you."

"Fine. I'm granting you entry. But only because I don't want you standing on my threshold and conjuring all manner of gossip. We've had enough of that in recent weeks. And I'm warming up the garden instead of the house with the door standing wide open. I'm Frances." She grumbled over her shoulder as she wedged them in.

"You're the nurse. My father speaks highly of you."

"Yes, I've assisted him on several deliveries. But flattery will get you nowhere. Arie and I have that in common."

She crossed her arms. "Tell me exactly what it is you want."

"I want Arie beside me. I want her out of that house that's shredding her soul."

"We all want the same thing, then." She acknowledged with a firm nod. "How do you propose to make that happen?"

"I think you and the rest of her sisters have to convince her."

"We've tried. Again and again. She doesn't hear our protests and believes she's still responsible for our health and well-being. Even though we're grown women and we manage just fine."

"Are you able to request a family meeting, or an intervention of some sort?"

"I could do that."

"But?"

"I need to make sure you don't want her for selfish reasons. She deserves to be cherished. Is that something you want to do or is the fact that she's good with children and capable of managing a household the thing that's the most appealing to you?"

"I came to your threshold of my own free will. I could find someone to mother my children if that's the only thing I sought." He twisted his cap in his hands, his expression agonized. "But now I truly know her and she's more than the girl I saw at her mother's deathbed. She's more than the widow of the loathsome squire and the ward of his equally loathsome heir. She's more than drudgery and sacrifice and invisibility. She's everything and I want her to see what the rest of us see when we look at her."

Some of Frances's ice had thawed at his impassioned outburst. She cleared her throat. "And what exactly is it that everyone sees when they look at her?"

"They see her giving. Again and again and again. And never asking for anything in return. I want to give her something in return. I want to bring her hot tea and let her sleep in. I want her to do whatever makes her happy – because she's never felt she's at leisure to do that."

"Then you want exactly what we want for her. I'll see what I can do."

"That's all I ask." He bowed his head and turned on his heel.

Frances flicked the corner of the curtains open and watched him walk away. She sighed. If only her own indulgence had been willing to make the same declaration. If only the smoke and guns of war hadn't driven a wedge between them and left her stranded here dreaming about what could have been. She was expecting a response from Nightingale's new hospital any day now and she hoped throwing herself into a new position would make it easier to forget him.

Gone Are Your Old Ideas of Life

"We want you to be happy more than we want his measly fifty pounds!" cried Cecily. She was the most exuberant of Arie's sisters. She'd barely been a year old when their mother had passed. She was now nearly twenty-six , the same age Arie had been when she was bartered to the squire. She'd pledged her troth at sixteen to a soldier and had been a widow for five years.

"You don't know what you're saying," argued Arie. "If you and Alec had received that fifty pounds you might not have had to move back into this house when he died," she grabbed her hand. "Fifty pounds will ensure your married lives begin with something. Some way to make the burden lighter. It's nothing to scoff at."

"It's something to scoff at if it means you're turning your back on love!" argued Gertrude. She was constantly pestering the lending library to stock more romances, so her protest was in character. She had dreams of writing penny dreadfuls.

"None of us need that money, Arie," reiterated Cecily. "Lavinia's happy apprenticing to the apothecary, Emily's been corresponding with that female detective in London, Jessamine likes being the village schoolteacher and Frances likes being a nurse. She's waiting on a letter inviting her to Nightingale's St. Thomas's Hospital."

"We don't need you to take care of us, Arie," Gertrude assured her. "You've been doing it your entire life. It's time you took care of yourself instead."

"She's correct," chimed in Cecily. "Violet Greaves is a terrible excuse for a human being. She reminds us of that awful Caroline Bingley in *Pride and Prejudice*."

"She pays no attention whatsoever to her daughters," Arie protested. "They need me, even if my sisters claim they don't need the money I was promised for their benefit," she stiffly concluded.

"None of that lot pay attention to their offspring. She's no different than her peers. The girls will be fine because they have money and connections. And even if you're not residing in the household, you can still be their friend and mentor."

"Cecily, if I left the household I don't think Hugh would allow any contact between us."

"You've been an important part of their lives and they seem extraordinarily resourceful. Especially Ruby. They'll find a way to maintain contact on their own, whether their father forbids it or not."

"She's right," Gertrude agreed. "You're making excuses. It's very obvious to us that you've a chance to make a life with someone who returns your sentiments. As long as he's not the type to dictate your every move, you should set aside your misgivings."

"You're coming to church tomorrow and you're going to look your best. We're of a size and I still have some of my outfits from London packed away in my trunk." Cecily grabbed her hand. "And you're going to wear one of them and drive him out of his mind. I have a gorgeous sarcenet blouse and garnet wool skirt that will make you even more irresistible."

Here You Are, Standing There, Loving Me

He stopped in front of her. She knew he was going to be immovable. His jaw was clenched and the fire she couldn't stop thinking about was in his eyes when he looked down at her.

They were standing in the churchyard and the other parishioners either scurried around them or stopped to gape. When she'd avoided his presence and overtures, the village had assumed there was no credence to the rumors. She had resumed her Sunday morning posts in the pew, her hands clasped in prayer, her expression implacable. And the rumor mill had turned to other things. How unwise her sister Frances was to hie off for London where it was much harder to breathe than it was here in the country. How her younger widowed sister Cecily had accepted the employment offer she received from one of her husband's former comrades in arms and was even now meandering her way to Inverness via the new rail line.

"Why are you accosting me now?" She demanded. "You couldn't even muster the courage to look at me in church today. Even though the twins weren't shy about sliding across the aisle to embrace me as soon as our eyes met and Clem and Claire wouldn't let go of my waist." She hoped her tone wasn't as bitter as it sounded to her own ears.

She'd missed the way he lifted his daughters to his shoulders when they complained of exhaustion. Even when they'd been frolicking minutes before, and it was obvious they just liked seeing the world from an exalted vantage point. She'd missed the hint of peppermint on his breath in the mornings after his ablutions, when he'd kissed her before they went about their day. She wanted to go sailing over the snow in a sleigh with him. She wanted to walk by his side through the orchard in the spring and feel the flutter of apple blossoms against her face as the breeze sent them dancing in the air.

"If I looked at you, I was going to stand up in the middle of the sermon, throw you over my shoulder and bring you somewhere we could have privacy."

"I see you're still finding it hard to control your base urges," she was somewhat mollified by his confession but still angry that it'd been more than two weeks with no overtures.

He gave her a rueful grin. "Around you, I'm always fighting my base urges. And I'm tired of fighting them. I want to surrender to them. I want to publicly claim you. But if I do that, if you consent to wed me, you'll be vulnerable to censure. I want to share all the details of my life with you, but I'm frightened it won't be enough. I'm scared I'm not enough to keep you happy," he stepped even closer, oblivious to the rapt audience.

She hadn't been able to find enough pins to coil her hair this morning, and he brushed his hand down the length of her braid. "You deserve to be happy, vixen. Your life thus far has been anything but."

"What if I've finally decided that being happy is what I deserve? What if I've finally realized the only time I've ever been truly happy is lying in your arms?" she quietly asked.

He searched her face, as if trying to verify her sincerity. "I need to be sure I understand what you're saying. That you know what the consequences of our union will be. Your stepson will never condone it and he'll forbid you from having any contact with his daughters. I know you love them as if they were your own and you fear the neglect they'll suffer if you're not there to intervene."

"I don't need Hugh's permission to be with you. I'm a woman of a certain age, and beyond his control. And the girls and I will find a way to see each other."

"What about your sisters?"

"I spoke with them. They assured me that the last thing they wanted was my sacrifice. They've all found their own paths, and they don't need my assistance or my interference."

"Then I don't have to wait to show you how much I've missed you," he swooped her up in his arms to the outraged gasps of those who wanted to see the drama unfold.

"Where are we going?" She breathlessly asked as she tucked her face against his chest.

"I'm taking you to St. Simon House."

"You're kidnapping me?"

"If that's what you choose to call it, then yes I'm kidnapping you."

The rough texture of his response sent a shiver up her spine. He unpeeled his hands long enough to seat her astride his horse before he swung up behind her. He clicked and tapped his heels against his mount's flanks and they were cantering down the main thoroughfare.

"We just caused the scandal of the decade." She didn't feel in the least ashamed of the spectacle they'd left in their wake.

The roads were finally cleared and their course was far smoother than the first one that brought her to his door.

They came to a halt in front of his stables and he dismounted. She twisted her body to follow him down and he shook his head. "No," was all he said before he swept her into his arms again.

The wind was brisk and he was warm, so she let him do it.

He stopped in front of the third stall and set her on her feet.

"Why are we stopping here?"

"Because there's something I think you should have."

"Does it involve bare skin?" She provocatively asked as she slid a finger down the bristle of his cheek.

"Not yet. But don't rule it out. I haven't named this filly, because I want you to do the honors."

"Why do you want me to name her?"

"Because I'm giving her to you."

"Is she a bribe?"

"No, she's not a bribe. If you decide not to marry me, she'll still be yours. No matter where you're living."

"Are you giving her to me because of the story I told you that first night in the hay?"

"Yes. And because no one should have had the power to separate you from Fireflower or sever that bond. I will never do that."

She crouched down and tapped her fingers against the railing. "Come here, little beauty."

The foal sniffed at her open palm and then nuzzled it. Arie brushed her hand over the satiny nose and sighed. "I have to name you Fireflower. You have a chestnut coat just like hers. But you're a treasure of your very own and I'll cherish you."

She stood and swiped her hands against her skirts, her eyes glowing with unshed tears.

"You're happy?" He tentatively asked.

A sob escaped her throat and she threw herself into his arms. "How could I not be? How do you always know what to do to ensure that I am? No one else makes me cry like this. Thank you."

"I have something else I want to show you. And it will involve bare skin."

"Mmm," she murmured. "I like your surprises."

He swept her into his arms again and carried her into the tack room. There was a saddle perched on the lone sawhorse, and that's where he deposited her.

She was seated astride it backwards and the uncomfortable dig of the pommel in the small of her back made her squirm. He reached for the shelf behind them and wedged a blanket roll in the spot, providing a cushion for her to recline against. He unfastened the tapes at her waist, coaxed her to raise her arms, and pulled the skirt over her head.

She sat there in her shirtwaist, decorously buttoned from her midriff up. But her pantaloons were spread wide. He placed her feet in the saddle stirrups, and she was even more open to his gaze. She couldn't decide if she wanted to recline and wait for his next move or reach between her legs and slide her own fingers through her folds.

She decided to do the latter. Hot gaze on him, she lowered her hand. She'd been priming herself with memories of what it felt like to be tied up in his bed, and she moaned as her fingers stroked through her wetness. She shivered as her thumb grazed the clitoris hidden by the hood of her sex.

"Whatever shall you do with me?" she teased. And then decided to indulge in one of her most prurient fantasies. "Highwaymen don't abduct virtuous women for no reason."

His eyes flared and she held her breath, wondering if he'd play along. He reached toward her, skating a finger down the smooth skin of her inner thigh. "Mayhap highwaymen aren't interested in virtuous women," he splayed his broad hand across her knee. "Mayhap highwaymen like women with a streak of naughty in their veins."

He cupped his fingers over her own, plunging them deeper, stroking the channel obscured by her labia. "I think you have a streak of naughty in your veins. I think you're rejoicing I captured you because you saw the way I handled a pistol and you imagined that's the way I handled my cock."

Obviously, he was willing to indulge her little fantasy. "Is that why you're about to tup me on your saddle? Because you like to think about me imagining your hand on your cock? Because you like to think about me wet and aching for your touch?"

"Who said I'm about to tup you? Mayhap I want to see your bare arse writhe against the leather of the saddle. Mayhap I want to see your body arch up in those stirrups when I use my teeth on your rosy nipples."

His hands fumbled at her throat, trying to dislodge the simple cameo pinned at the top of her shirt. "Dammit." He managed to unclasp it, but a bright drop of blood welled on his thumb. She grasped it and lifted his hand to her mouth. She licked it away, letting her lips rest there for a moment to soothe it.

His eyes were half-lidded as he watched her. He gently extracted his hand and bent diligently over the row of buttons. "It should not arouse me so much to see you acting like a carnivorous kitten." He growled. "I've been dreaming of the bounty behind these buttons."

In that moment she was grateful beyond measure that all her dresses buttoned up the front so she could easily don her garments. After what seemed like a thousand years but was most likely no more than a handful of seconds, his broad palms slipped to her side. She could feel the heat of his touch seeping through her chemise, two brands that shaped the outer curve of her breasts. Her eyes met his and followed his gaze as he glanced down and seemed mesmerized. She couldn't stop her nipples from peaking at the molten desire she saw.

"You are the stuff of dreams." He hoarsely muttered. "Proof that somewhere in my misspent youth, and despite all my sins, I did something good."

She watched, utterly entranced, and completely transfixed, as the rough pad of one thumb brushed across the cotton clinging to her straining breast. She arched toward him, desperate for more of that firm, yet gentle, touch. "You have the most mouth-watering tits I've ever seen." He murmured reverently. "I know they're silky and sweet. I know they'll be more decadent on my tongue than sweet Belgian chocolate. I want to lick them and rub my day's growth of beard all over them. And then place my cock between them while you take me in your mouth."

His blatant confession sent a swirl of heat spiraling from her navel to her core. "I don't care if this shift is disintegrated or destroyed. I need your hands and your mouth on me now."

He ripped her cotton chemise straight down the middle and situated her further into the saddle seat. She arched her back as his mouth whispered over her and couldn't stop the moans as he covered the entirety of one breast with his hand and mouth, lashing it with his tongue, nipping it with his teeth, and then suckling it as she rubbed against him. He skated the tip of his nose down the long, arched curve of her neck and the hot staccato cadence of his breath throbbed against her pulse.

"I have a surprise for you, Arie," he rasped into her neck.

"Another one?" She gasped. She didn't know how many more of his surprises her heart or her body could take.

He stepped back and extracted one of the most intriguing devices she'd ever seen from his pocket. "What is that?" she asked. She knew what it looked like. But she couldn't believe he'd procured one. She'd seen pictures in the naughty books she'd found, but she'd never thought to behold a real one. "Is that what I think it is?" She asked as her eyes roved over the wooden knob with a crank and gears affixed to its handle. She'd seen a crude drawing in one of the books in the squire's salacious collection.

"It's marketed as a cure for women's hysteria. Which we both know is an excuse to ignore the medical problems of your gender, or the desire to pursue anything beyond a traditional role. But that's not what most couples use it for," he explained with a sinful grin.

He wrapped his fingers around the crank and turned it until the knob was rotating at a vigorous speed. And then he dropped to his knees in front of her, his mouth even with her sex.

He slid the device inside her and let his tongue flutter against her clitoris in a steady rhythm.

"How do you even know about such things?" she barely managed to gasp out.

He raised his head to answer her questions. "As I've said, Rachel and I enjoyed experimenting. And a soldier on the Continent hears things. They say the Chinese have invented all manner of pleasure tools."

He lowered his head, and the delicate bombardment of his tongue nearly made her forget her name. The vibrations from the toy slowed, and then stopped completely. He nipped her clit with the edge of his molars, and she rose in the saddle, her legs quaking. Lost in sensation as euphoria swept through her veins.

He rumbled into her sex, swirling his tongue and lapping up her arousal.

He stood when her legs finally stopped quivering. He kept his gaze on her as he unbuttoned his breeches, pulling them down just far enough to free his cock. "I won't last," he warned.

He lifted her from the saddle and carried her to the wall. He slid inside, one hand bracketing her hip like a manacle, his head bowed into the crease between her neck and her shoulder.

He pistoned inside her like a man lost, rubbed his beard against her skin like he was a recalcitrant puppy seeking benediction, and roared as he came. She rested her palm against his nape. He'd let go of his reluctance, or she'd moved him beyond caring. She could feel his semen leaking outside her body and she wanted to clamp her legs together to keep it there.

"Does the fact you just gave me one of your precious horses and made me see stars against this barn wall mean you're mine?" she asked.

"I've been yours from the first moment I saw you on the steps of the church. I buried it because I loved my wife. Because I loved you in a way I didn't love her. Our love was borne of growing up together, and long-time affection, but the way I feel about you. It's like I'll starve if I don't have you in my arms. I think it started when your mother died. Something in you called to something in me and it never wavered, it just grew." He dropped his hands from the wall behind her and smoothed his palms over the curves of her cheekbones. Her legs slid to the floor of their own accord.

"There is nothing tame or quiet about my feelings for you." He assured her.

"What are your feelings for me? You haven't exactly spelled them out." Suspicion wasn't knowledge and she needed to hear the affirmation. He'd said everything but those three words and she needed to hear them. Maybe then she'd take the plunge and risk saying them back.

"I love you, you daft woman. Every stubborn, infuriating, gorgeous inch of you."

No one else saw how obstinate she could be, and she loved that she was able to get under his skin. "I love you too, you blockheaded, incorrigible, glorious man."

NOTE TO READER

Prior to the Wills Act of 1837, a widow was entitled to a portion of her deceased husband's estate until her death or remarriage. The fifty pounds Arie wants Hugh to bestow on her sisters might not sound like a lot, but the average salary of a servant in an upper-class London home in 1861 was only ten to fifteen pounds a year. That money would likely go a lot further in the countryside where bartering was more common. The views espoused by Hugh were prevalent at the time, and his treatment of his stepmother would have been regarded as benevolent.

On the use of hand-cranked vibrators... yes, they were both prevalent and popular throughout the Victorian Age. And likely before. The French invented a device called the "tremoussoir" in 1734. It functioned with a wind-up key. The vibrator Thaddeus uses on Arie was inspired by both this early version and Macaura's Pulsocon, which was available in the Sears Roebuck catalog until the 1920s.

I wanted this story to reflect as much of the setting of a true Victorian Christmas celebration as possible. Most of the traditions we associate with our modern celebrations had their roots in the decade between 1810-1820, and many were hallmarks of the German festivities brought over by the Hanoverian court. These traditions became further entrenched with the publication of Dickens' Christmas Carol in the 1840s.

There were a couple of things I was unable to verify. Although Clement Moore's poem was published in 1830, I couldn't definitively pinpoint when its depiction of Santa Claus was adopted across the pond. Our story is set in 1861, so I'm going to assume widespread adoption was common.

I couldn't verify what type of conifer was typically used for trees, as the Scottish conifer forests were decimated by shipbuilding and hadn't yet recovered.

I couldn't verify that Devon Longwools were being raised in the Cumbrian region, but I took some license as they were rising in popularity due to the quality of their wool and the exponential growth of the textile industry. Cumbria is located in the lake district, and its hilly terrain wasn't ideally suited for large scale farming at the time. Many farmers turned to livestock such as sheep that could thrive as foragers.

Stay tuned for the next book in the series. It will be the story of Arie's sister Frances. She does receive her letter from the St. Thomas Hospital, and she accepts the appointment. And comes face to face with the autocratic doctor she worked alongside on the blood-soaked battlefields of the Crimean War. It's inspired by my love of House and Grey's Anatomy and I can't wait for you to read it!

ACKNOWLEDGEMENTS

As always, thank you to my very own tea-bringer, my husband Anthony. He's my rock and my bridge and my soulmate. He gets when I'm distracted because I have a million and one ideas trying to burst out of my head and onto the page like flying monkeys. He gets it when I need peace and quiet and wine and coffee. He's my sounding board and he supports every dream I've ever had. And the ones I don't even know about yet.

Thank you to all my ARC and beta readers – you make my journey so much easier.

Thank you to all the authors who have reached out and offered support and advice. I'm in awe of your knowledge and appreciate your kindness.

Thank you to every single one of you who picks up this book. Please consider leaving a review on Amazon, Goodreads or the platform of your choice. Good or bad, your impressions and opinions help me grow in my craft and I appreciate every single one.

About the Author

I have been reading historical romance for thirty-eight years, and I've always wanted to explore the stories of those who led ordinary lives in extraordinary times.

I love cravats and carriages and crinolines and obscure slang and delving into the intricacies of historical flourishes and furbelows.

A list of all the authors whose words I've devoured would probably wrap twice around the world.

Literacy and having the freedom to read what we want to read is something I will never take for granted. It would mean the world to me if you thought about donating to Pen America's efforts to battle the banning of books in school libraries.

I also write very steamy, small town contemporary romance and paranormal, shapeshifter romance inspired by Scottish water horse mythology and folklore.

You can follow me or leave a review on Goodreads here: https://www.goodreads.com/author/show/22315243.Andrea_Je nelle

You can join the private Facebook Group, The Willow Creek Wantons, to access giveaways and participate in readalongs, here: https://www.facebook.com/groups/485062863815949/

www.ingramcontent.com/pod-product-compliance
Lightning Source LLC
Chambersburg PA
CBHW060410310726

48976CB00003B/999